PULP
Literature

PULP *Literature*

Pulp Literature Press

Issue No. 41, Winter 2024

Publisher: Pulp Literature Press; Editor-in-Chief: Jennifer Landels; Senior Editor: Mel Anastasiou; Acquisitions Editor: Genevieve Wynand; Poetry Editors: Daniel Cowper & Emily Osborne; Assistant Editors: Brooklynn Hook, Sierra Louie, Ellen Spacey; Copy Editor: Amanda Bidnall; Proofreader: Sierra Louie; Graphic Design: Amanda Bidnall & Sierra Louie; Cover Design: Kate Landels; Subscriptions: Carol McCauley & Brooklynn Hook; Advertising: Brooklynn Hook. For advertising rates, direct inquiries to info@pulpliterature.com.

Cover painting, *Cheers* by Melissa Mary Duncan. Illustration for 'Get Home Safe' by Sierra Louie. All other illustrations by Mel Anastasiou.

Pulp Literature: ISSN 2292-2164 (Print), ISSN 2292-2172 (Digital), Issue No. 41, Winter 2024.

Pulp Literature Press is based in the unceded traditional Coast Salish Territories of the Katzie, Kwantlen, Matsqui, and Semiahmoo First Nations.

Pulp Literature Press gratefully acknowledges the support of the Canada Council for the Arts and the Government of Canada.

Pulp Literature is a proud member of the Magazine Association of BC and Magazines Canada.

TABLE OF CONTENTS

FROM THE PULP LIT PULPIT

The Next Chapter

Winter is the bookend season of our yearly calendar. In the northern hemisphere, January opens in winter, and with winter again, each spent year closes. At the toll of midnight on New Year's Eve, in that suspended moment between ending and beginning, we stare into the two faces of 'resolution': something is solved; something is promised.

With this issue we are celebrating not just the start of a new year, but a new decade as well. In our previous edition, we tipped our hat to the first forty (forty!) issues. And now we begin again with the first of whatever the future has in store. All of this got me to thinking about beginnings and, not endings per se, but continuings. So, in preparation for this editorial, I surveyed a few members of the *Pulp* team: What got you started with the magazine? What keeps you going?

For our OGs, it was, and still is, all about the magic of curation and creation. As Mel told me, her *Pulp* inspo began and continues with "printing the stories we like to read." And for Jen, "the thrill of holding the new print proof, of having birthed something that is beautiful, never gets old."

For two of our newer members, the now fully birthed magazine was itself the draw. Brooklynn joined us while the world was neck deep in a pandemic, and engaging with the magazine's "fabulous, weird, and absorbing works" was a wonderful way to learn the ins and outs of publishing. For

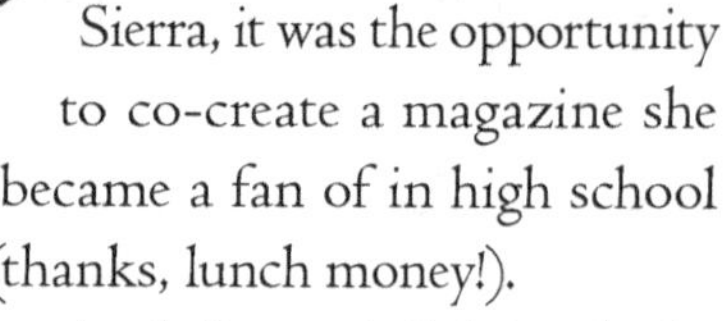

Sierra, it was the opportunity to co-create a magazine she became a fan of in high school (thanks, lunch money!).

And for me? I joined the magazine around its midway-to-now point: five years ago. What got me started was the opportunity to dive deep into the world of editing. What keeps me going? The incredible community of *Pulp Literature* writers, editors, and readers.

This magazine began when three women, united in their shared love of the written word, created a space where both emerging and established writers could find a home for their work. All of us, founders and newbies alike, continue to delight in stumbling upon a hidden gem of a story from a first-time writer, and in introducing a noted author to a whole new audience. And to witness and support an author's journey from 'emerging' to 'established'? There's nothing quite like it.

As so many of these developing writers remind us, whatever your newfound passion, it doesn't matter *when* you start; it matters *that* you start. Ten years and forty issues later, we're so glad they did.

~Genevieve Wynand

Join us as we raise a glass to the New Year and a new decade with *Cheers* by cover artist **Melissa Mary Duncan**.

Ghosts rise from the depths of different pasts to haunt the pages of 'When Captain Picard Was My Dad' by feature author **Finnian Burnett** and 'The Haunted Ghost' by **JJ Lee**.

Family both anchors and unmoors the varied casts of 'Moon Eater' by **EC Dorgan**, 'Field's Nocturne No. 10 in E Major' by **Matt Lumbard**, and 'The Golden Bull' by **JM Landels**.

Time and space rattle and quake in 'Nobody Knows It but Me' by **Franco Amati** and 'Separate Worlds' by **Chip Houser**. And the shattering continues with new poetry from **Aaron Poochigian**, **DS Maolalai**, and **Purbasha Roy**.

But journeys finally find peace in the destination with 'Get Home Safe' by **Sierra Louie** and 'Stella Ryman and the Labyrinthian Puzzle' by **Mel Anastasiou**.

WHEN CAPTAIN PICARD WAS MY DAD

Finnian Burnett

Finnian Burnett *holds a doctoral degree in English pedagogy and teaches English online for a US college. Their writing explores intersections of identity—fatness, mental health, disability, queer joy. Finnian was a finalist for the 2023 CBC Nonfiction Prize. Their second novella-in-flash,* The Price of Cookies, *is available from Off Topic Publishing. Finnian lives in BC where they spend their time watching a lot of* Star Trek *and daydreaming about teleportation.*

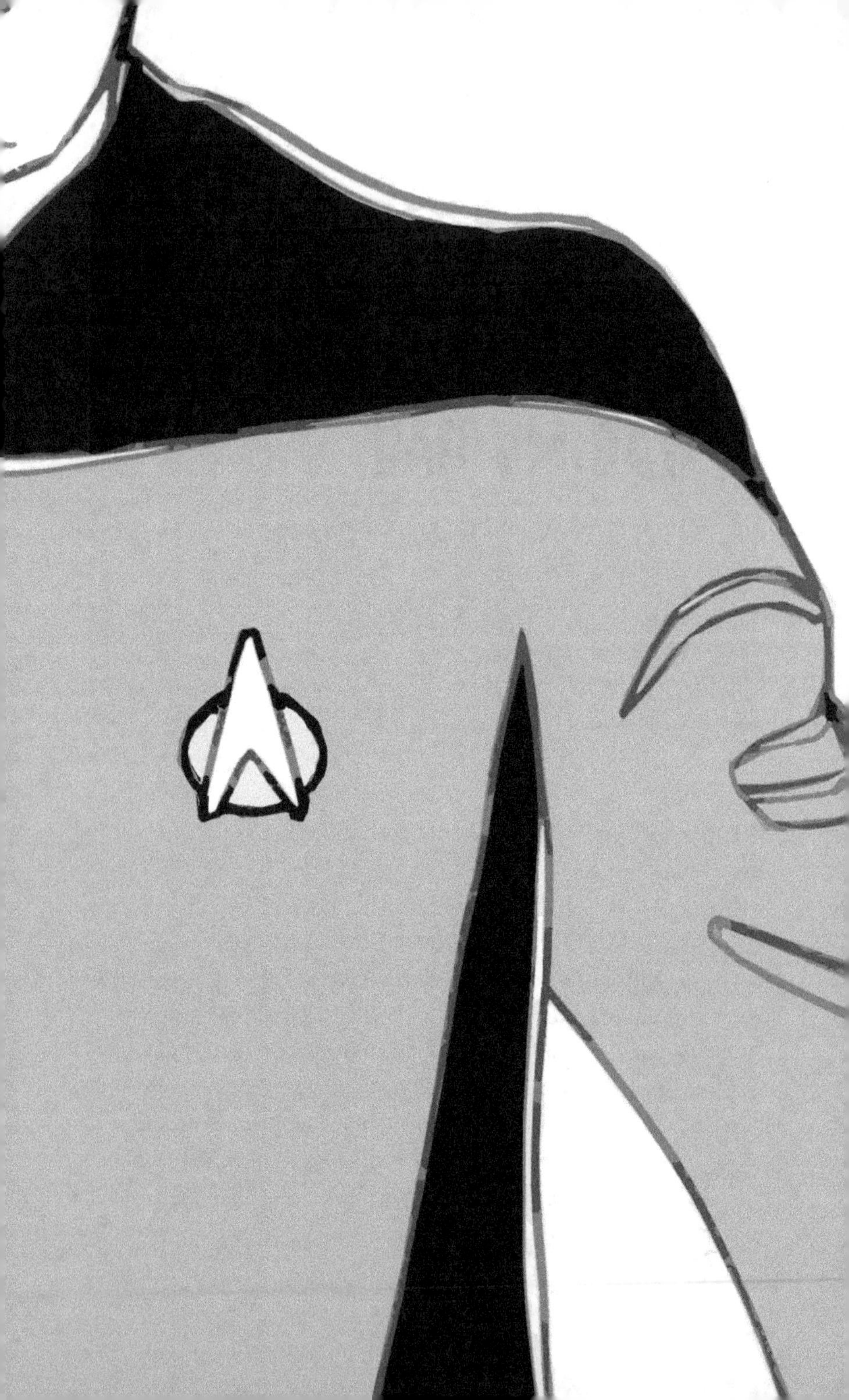

When Captain Picard Was My Dad

When I didn't make the kickball team, Captain Picard didn't say, "I'd hoped at least one of my kids wasn't a loser." He didn't say that at all. He didn't tell me I'd make the team next year if I lost some weight because an oinker like me couldn't keep up with the other third-graders. Captain Picard told me that you can do your best and still lose and that he believed I did my best. He said I should be proud of myself, even if no one else was proud of me.

When Captain Picard was my dad, I didn't get beaten with a yardstick after I was suspended in the fourth grade. I didn't get thrown into my bedroom without dinner and I didn't lie awake all night to the throbbing of my burgeoning bruises. After all, when Will Riker violated the Treaty of Algernon, Captain Picard told him that the important thing was not what he did in the past but what he did going forward. Will almost started a war with the Romulans, and all I did was write 'fuck school' on the wall of the second-floor bathroom outside the chemistry lab, but Captain Picard forgave us either way.

Captain Picard never said fat girls should have nicer personalities and fat girls don't have to be strong because they can sit on their enemies, and he never, ever said 'whoa, my god, it's coming towards me'. Captain Picard never smashed my head into the garage door or pulled out a handful of my hair or threw the remote at me so hard it left a scar on my eyebrow. And when Captain Picard was my dad, I didn't wear long sleeves and jeans in the summer.

When Captain Picard was my dad, I didn't have to sit at the bedside of someone I hated, didn't hear the skeleton breath of someone who was dying but not fast enough, didn't bite my tongue as my dead name rattled again and again from bone-dry lips. I didn't clutch my arms against my sides to keep anxiety from eating me alive. I didn't pretend the scars disappeared with the bruises. I didn't have to do it, none of it, not when Captain Picard was my dad.

FEATURE INTERVIEW

Finnian Burnett

Pulp Literature: *'When Captain Picard Was My Dad' is, to say the least, incredibly powerful. The raw undercurrents lie just beneath the immaculately crafted surface. And it feels like the emotional impact hits so hard not despite the story's brevity but because of it. Could you tell us about the creation and crafting of this piece?*

Finnian Burnett: I've been working on a whole novella of *Star Trek*-themed flash fiction stories. I think people are expecting science fiction when I say that, but really the stories are all about contemporary people, dealing with the challenges of life, who get inspiration or healing from *Star Trek*. This was one of the first stories because I remember watching *The Next Generation* in high school and thinking Captain Picard was so fair, even when he was angry. I thought he would never raise his hand to a kid, never make them feel dismissed or afraid. I wanted to capture that longing for a home life that some kids don't experience, the way we transfer our feelings onto a character who doesn't actually exist and probably wouldn't be perfect if they did.

PL: *With your stories, you do so very much in so very few words. In the process of writing flash fiction, do you 'write big' and then scale back, or is the concision part of the process?*

FB: The contrary! I almost always 'write small' and go back to flesh out the details. Short form comes naturally to me — writing longer form stories now seems like scaling a mountain. I was asked to submit to an anthology with a per-story word count of 5,000 and I was like, really? What am I going to waffle on about for so many words?

PL: *For this, our tenth-anniversary issue, we've been reflecting on what got us started and what keeps us going. And so I ask, what got you started in the world of flash fiction? What keeps you going?*

FB: I was dealing with a lot — a bad bout in my depression, trying to maintain teaching full-time college classes, going to grad school, running an online writing academy, Covid lockdowns, breathing now and then. I hadn't worked on a novel in a couple of years because I was giving energy to everything but my own writing. And a friend sent me a link for a class given by Grace Palmer, a UK-based writer, on writing flash fiction. The idea of brevity appealed to me and I loved the idea that I could write something in maybe twenty minutes and feel I'd accomplished something. The class generated some stories that had me long-listing, then shortlisting, in some contests, and I was hooked.

I keep going because it's a way out of the slumps. Maybe I haven't written in a couple weeks but I'll suddenly sit down and write a flash piece in twenty minutes, and no matter what else happens that day, I've written. And it turns out all those little flash pieces can add to a larger work. I've published one novella-in-flash and I have another one coming out this year. And the novel I'm currently working on is mostly told through short-form, interconnected scenes.

PL: *What do you find are the biggest challenges with this ultra-short form of storytelling?*

FB: Giving readers a sense of satisfaction at the end. Flash, perhaps more than any other style of writing, must make the reader do a lot of the work. A lot of the time, the story is in the in-betweens, in the movement, rather than in a traditional arc. People who are used to reading beats with rising action that culminates in a climax and a denouement may find some flash stories feel unfinished. I try to ensure I'm giving my readers a sense of completion, an understanding that it's over, even if there isn't a standard ending.

PL: *Who are your trusted first readers?*

FB: Author Andrew Shaugnessy. He's my go-to because he gets my voice, but he also has an innate ability to see what I was trying to do and to point out when I didn't quite get there. Also, his feedback is so compassionate and gentle, while also getting right to the heart of it. My wife, August, is also an excellent first reader, but because she knows me so well, she often knows what I *meant* even if it doesn't come across clearly on the page.

PL: *Among other themes, your work explores identity, reinvention, and self-discovery. These universal journeys are enacted through very specific, mostly-silenced-until-now bodies and voices. It is a remarkable magic that you create——uniting readers in our fundamental human-ness. When writing, do you envision a particular reader or audience? Or do you intentionally cast a net wide enough to scoop up the multitudes?*

FB: Octavia Butler said something about writing being one of the only professions where you can psychoanalyze yourself in public and get paid for it. So, first, I tap into my own feelings, the unhealed places that still need to be unpacked. I've found that even when I'm writing about a certain identity, people can still relate because some themes, such as isolation, feeling othered, balancing between forgiveness and rage at injustices, are universal. I think that's my main goal — to write about identities and bodies that are important to me, but to relate to anyone who's ever felt othered in any way.

PL: *You were recently shortlisted for the 2023 CBC nonfiction prize for your story 'That Poor Girl'. Congratulations! Could you tell us about the experience of writing and submitting the piece, and then later getting the news?*

FB: I'm still reeling from this. It felt huge and a little over-whelming. For a while, my email in-box and my social media private messages were just scrolling with people congratulating me. That story tapped into something I don't like to talk about with anyone but my older sister — our father as a predator. I first dashed off a draft of that, maybe 200 words or so, and sent it to my sister, who said it felt unfinished. It was unfinished because I was afraid to dive too deep into it. I set it aside and didn't think about it again for months. And then one day, I was browsing my unfinished stories folder and I pulled it out and wrote the rest of it, all in a blur, maybe in fifteen minutes. I edited a little for typos and grammar, but other than that, I didn't do any revisions, and it's one of the few stories I didn't send to a beta reader before submitting. I think I was worried I'd lose my nerve if I didn't submit immediately, so I did.

When I got the email that I had longlisted, I hovered in this strange space between absolutely elated and absolutely horrified. The idea of people reading my family's dirty laundry! I remember saying to my friend Andrew that I wish I had just called it fiction and submitted it to the fiction contest. But he told me people needed to hear the story and he was right. After it was published, the number of emails I got from people on their own healing journeys both broke my heart and bolstered my confidence that I'd made the right decision to submit it to such a huge platform.

PL: *Thank you for making the time to speak with us. Before we go, tell us, what are you working on now?*

FB: Thank you for asking me! I'm working on so much right now. I finished grad school and have settled back into my own writing. I'm having the most delightful time co-writing a speculative dark comedy novel with my friend Andrew Buckley. We're having a great time with it—spend most of our planning meetings giggling. I'm also working on an epistolary novel about Arthur, the trans man character from *The Clothes Make the Man*. I got a Canada Council for the Arts grant for this one, which means I get to go to London to research it. So it feels huge and important and it's slow-going. And I'm polishing the last few stories for a collection of queer love stories that I'll be shopping soon.

Select Bibliography

The Price of Cookies, Off Topic Publishing, forthcoming
The Clothes Make the Man, Ad Hoc Fiction, 2023
Coyote Ate the Stars (as EA Van Stralen), 2018

THE GOLDEN BULL

JM Landels

JM Landels is the author of the bestselling Allaigna's Song trilogy as well as the spy novel The Shepherdess, *currently serialized in even-numbered issues of this magazine. 'The Golden Calf', featured in Pulp Literature Issue 39, was a crossover of sorts, set in Allaigna's world of the Ilmar but with the Shepherdess's metier of herding livestock. 'The Golden Bull' finds the same character, nineteen years later, facing a different sort of burden. JM herself stays away from ruminants but does keep a small herd of horses on which she teaches mounted combat at her school, Academie Cavallo, in Langley, BC. You can find @jmlandels on most social media platforms, or at jmlandels.stiffbunnies.com.*

The Golden Bull

Saoira looks her son up and down, hands on hips. At eighteen summers old, Lennis has exceeded both his parents' height. His bronze curls and burnished skin, over the muscles of a farmhand, make him look like a statue from the Imperial Age, fit to grace the Duchess's hall in Rillonna. But it is a different duchy he is going to.

Saoira never told Allenis Andreg, Duke of Teillai, that he fathered a son the last time he visited her. Their correspondence has continued since Allenis's marriage, and Saoira has indeed mentioned her son. But though she has made no mention of a husband or another lover, Allenis has never inquired. He must at least suspect the boy is his, which may be why he continues to overpay for his thrice-yearly order of cheese. His daughters and his other sons have grown up on Little Water Ash, just as Lennis has.

"Why Teillai?" she demands. "Rillonna is closer, as is Doniver."

"Teillai has the finest master of arms in all Aerach. I want to learn from the best."

Saoira shakes her head. He's never been able to lie to her, though not for lack of trying. "I know why you're going, love. I just want to hear you say it."

"Is it so wrong to want to see the face of my father?"

"And can you see his without him seeing yours? Without him learning your name?"

"I'll be a nameless, faceless guard in his garrison."

She knows he will be neither nameless nor faceless for long. His stunning looks and easy manner attract the attention of everyone he meets. She's no Leisanmira seer, but she can predict he'll rise through the ranks like cream to the top of jug. She doesn't say this.

Instead she says, "You must never reveal who your father is. To anyone." The curls on Lennis's head sit a hand and a half closer to the sky upon Lennis's tall frame, but anyone with a keen eye will recognize the broad face and wide-set eyes that crinkle to slits when he laughs—which is often. How can he not stand out?

Lennis's height did not come from the Duke, nor from Saoira's mother, for the Littles had always been, well, *little*. Until Saoira came along and outgrew her mother. Saoira knows nothing of her father, but she suspects he was Leisanmira. It would explain Lennis's height, as well as his gold-tinged hair and green eyes. Given the nomadic nature of the Leisanmira clans, it would also explain a father who never reappeared in her life. She long ago gave up asking, or even wondering about, her father. Perhaps she should have been as coy to Lennis as her mother had been to her. If he did not know his father was the Duke of Teillai, he would not be hying off to enlist in Allenis's garrison. She also acknowledges, with no small amount of regret, that she should have given her son a different name. But when the squally, wet creature first lay against her breast, she was overwhelmed by so many emotions that no other name seemed possible.

Saoira tries to evaluate her state of mind now. Worry, yes, that her child has chosen a life of violence — and that if his heritage becomes known it will endanger his career and possibly even his life. She does not think Lauresa of Teillai will look kindly on a bastard child of Allenis's, especially one senior to her own. But there is another feeling nestling in her heart, and it is, she finally admits to herself, envy. Though Allenis's letters continue to come, less frequently but no less earnestly than before, she has not seen his face since Lennis was conceived.

Still, through letters, Saoira has learned much of the Duke's household. She knows the names and ages of all his children. She suspects, but has not voiced, that his oldest daughter is not his at all, for he was frank with Saoira in those early days, and he wrote that he did not consummate his marriage till two weeks after the wedding. And yet the child, as he reported eight months later, was a fine and healthy weight, and gave her mother much difficulty in labour.

Lennis's birth was remarkably easy for a first calving. Saoira laboured in the byre amid her cattle, preferring to deliver her babe on fresh straw, which could be swept into the midden, rather than soil her bed. Her dairy-hand, Reeth, helped her, bringing tea and cool cloths, tying off the cord, and reminding her to push out the afterbirth when she was distracted and lovestruck by the tiny face nestled between her breasts.

It seems love also bloomed between Allenis and his wife, Lauresa, whether he suspected a cuckoo in his nest or not. Saoira could tell from the letters, which became fewer and more matter of fact, though they were full of praise for his wife. The next few children, a son and three more daughters, she felt sure were his. But that last son, so many years younger than the rest—him, she wasn't sure of.

Saoira couldn't pin down the character of Lauresa of Teillai. She was a beauty, as the troubadours would have it, but she never visited Rillonna and seldom even travelled to Prince Vishod's court at Aleran, so gossip was rare. Allenis never spoke ill of her, and Saoira could only tell if he and his wife were on good terms by Lauresa's absence or presence in his missives.

Saoira is sure, however, that she, not Lauresa, was Allenis's first love, though he didn't declare it till too late. It is both a comfort and a regret. Though she sometimes wonders about the life she would have had, had she accepted his offer of marriage. She is proud of her dairy in Little Water and can't imagine giving up her cattle to manage a castle.

But Lennis is young, and he wants what he feels should be his. Saoira has taught him as much of the manners of court as she knows; she has taught him figures and letters and even paid tutors for riding and fencing lessons. It felt proper that some of Allenis's generous coin should give his son at least part of a noble education. Perhaps that, as much as his parentage, gave Lennis the longing for a higher station. Either way, it is too late now to change his path. She can only hope she has imparted wisdom and caution to him as well.

When the first letter from Lennis arrives, Saoira's hands tremble from relief, making the paper hard to read.

> *I am well, Mother, and hope this finds you the same. I have accepted a position within the castle garrison and have begun my training . . .*

Her relief fades a bit. Why the castle? Would not the town be enough? The rest describes a daily routine that is rigorous but ultimately no challenge for a young man used to hiking up mountains, pitching hay, and wrestling calves at castrating time. There is nothing to worry her at all, and yet she feels as worried as ever.

Over the course of his first year away, Lennis writes as often as his father used to, and Saoira learns about Allenis's family all over again, now through her son's eyes. He has ingratiated himself, becoming training partners with his older half siblings, an assistant and companion to the family nurse, and a personal guard to Allenis's wife, Lauresa, all without revealing his parentage. Or so he claims. Saoira can read between the lines, and she worries about all that he does not see: that the eldest legitimate son's jealousy could grow deadly on the training ground if it were revealed they are half brothers. That the attentions his half-sister showers on him are the signs of a puppy love that absolutely must not be encouraged, even were they not blood relatives. That his glowing words about the mistress of the castle resemble Allenis's own when he is most in love with Lauresa.

Saoira is vague in her letters to her son and his father both. She does not name Allenis in her missives to Lennis, in case the letters should fall into other hands. And she does not tell Allenis that his son has left home — never mind that he has enlisted in Osthegn's garrison.

In her dreams, Saoira follows these figures, and watches her son embroil himself in far more political danger than any son of a cowherd could weather. And by day, her worry does not cease.

Buttercup, the bull calf that Allenis gave Saoira, or rather imposed upon her, when they first met, has defied all odds and lived longer than any bull known from Rillonna to Colvale. The delicate build she thought would be a liability kept him from growing to the size of her red-and-white mountain cattle, and in the end, saved his fine legs and hooves from breaking down under the weight that most bulls carry. His breeding days were done by the time Lennis was learning to count change in the creamery shop. But visits from tree-priests have kept the other ailments of age away, and at twenty-five he has outlived most of his offspring.

Around the time that Buttercup retired as a stud, Saoira bought the neighbouring farm from the family that leased him. He was back in her sole possession now that he was bringing in no coin at all. The sensible thing would have been to butcher him then.

In ancient times, bulls were symbols of prosperity and fertility, and were sacrificed to mythical deities. Radhan, her favourite tree-priest, told her there was some validity in the practice. "Blood magic works, but the days of sacrificing whole animals" — though she didn't say 'people', tree-priests make little distinction between humans and other vertebrates — "are gone. We can affect the same magic with our own vitality, willingly given and easily replenished." Saoira suspects, though, that there are greater magics than those modern Woodkin practise — and that there is a reason they are banned.

Despite the burden he is, Buttercup has brought enough wealth for her to not begrudge the increasing portion of her purse she spends to keep him. Allenis's support of her dairy has given her the capital to increase her holdings, improve her broodstock, and afford a few luxuries, like keeping an aged bull as a pet ... and running a farm without the help of a husband.

In the early winter, Saoira sends for Radhan. Buttercup has another hoof abscess — he's been prone to them for the last few years — and this one is stubborn. After the tree-priest has opened the sole to drain the pus, and applied a pad and her healing magic, Saoira invites her into the kitchen for the usual mug of hot perry.

"How much longer will you keep him going?" Radhan asks.

Saoira takes a sip, burning her tongue on the too-hot perry as she avoids answering the question she's asked herself every year for the past half dozen. She has put down many a cow in her long career, some for meat, some because of injury, and some to save the cost of another winter's feed for an old girl that no longer gives calves or milk.

But now that her son has gone away, this bull, the one she never wanted, is her only link to Allenis. At last, she answers with a shrug. "He seems content for the most part. You'd tell me if that were otherwise?" She glances at Radhan.

"He's comfortable now. And you have spent gold aplenty keeping him that way."

Saoira knows that the ever-increasing cost of Radhan's services doesn't enrich the tree-priest's coffers. It goes to the vast amounts of food — grain, eggs, fish roe, nuts, and cream — that fuels Woodkin magic. She has never seen a fat tree-priest. Radhan's cheeks are gaunt already, and there are still three moons till spring thaw. Saoira resolves to take another pound of Little Water butter from the cold room to give to her friend.

"How fares Lennis?" asks Radhan.

"His absence is a hole in my heart," she replies, and something about the warm perry after the long and worrying day makes her pour out her concerns — ones she'd not even shared with Reeth — to the tree-priest. As her litany draws to a close, a shadow of a thought crosses her wrung-out heart. "The charms you perform on my herd to ward off roundworms and wolves — can they work on us?"

Radhan gives her a gentle smile. "I assume you don't think he's in danger from parasites or predators."

"Only the human kind," replies Saoira. "I do not want his heritage coming to the attention of the court—the Duke's wife in particular. And, of course, I want him safe from the perils of warfare."

"I could cast a charm that would make him slide beneath the notice of others, but that might affect his chances of promotion. And if," Radhan makes a warding sign against her forehead, "war occurs, such a charm might make him a useful spy or scout but could prevent his comrades from noticing him if he falls on the field."

Radhan ponders the inside of her empty cup. "I could cast a spell that affects his perspicacity, to allow greater insight, make him more aware of danger, and help him navigate the pitfalls of court. But, like all my charms, it would wear off over time. I visit your herd four times a year, after all." She lowers her voice, even though they are alone in the kitchen. "Blood magic would make it last longer, but even at that, the body changes, grows older all the time, and the muscles, skin, and organs—even the bones—that have been enchanted are replaced entirely in six or seven years."

Six or seven years seems a good deal better than nothing, but Radhan seems to read her mind.

"And throughout that time, the effect would be constantly dwindling. Parts that heal faster, like skin and muscle, would be back to normal within a year. The teeth, however, would bear a trace of enchantment forever. Which sounds like a good thing, until you encounter a mage on the hunt for signs of blood magic. It would be a marker he'd carry around for life."

Just as Saoira feels the weight of defeat settle, she grasps at another straw. "What of enchanted items?" She has heard of tokens—rings, amulets, and the like—that carry enchantment with them, long past the grave.

Radhan shakes her head. "Most of those were made in the Lothlecan era. And what remain are held by princes and dukes, and very seldom sold."

Lotherasien magic, Saoira knows, is what caused the Cataclysm of centuries back. Blood magic may be banned, but the even more dangerous magic of the Empire has been deliberately lost.

After another silence, Radhan continues. "Leisanmira craftsmen have retained the secret of imbuing magic in materials. But I have never met a Leisanmira willing to perform blood magic. They are a persecuted people in most cities, hesitant to take risks with illicit magic."

"But tree-priests do," Saoira says. It should be a question but comes out like a challenge.

Radhan gives a slow nod. "When we have to. When our own bodies no longer sustain our work."

Saoira can't help but think Radhan is at that point now.

"I've missed you so, my dear."

It has been close to a year since Saoira's seen Lennis, her only flesh and blood. He smells the same as ever beneath the travel dust and strange clothes. She wraps her arms around him and notices he's thicker through the shoulders. And a finger-width taller, perhaps. But his bronze-gold curls and beautiful smile are the same as ever.

"And I you, Mother." His voice is formal, and deeper than she remembers. There's a catch of emotion in it, which brings back all of her worries over the past year. But she has a solution for that.

"Come," she says, and takes her towering son by the hand to lead him into the kitchen he grew up in.

She feeds him as much as he can eat — which is no small amount — and listens as he recounts his year. It is little more than he's told her in letters, but it is more intense. She feels his passion for the art of arms; his fondness for some of his unacknowledged half siblings; his wariness of others; his respect for Angeley, the family's nurse and gardener; and his attraction — which he tries to hide, but which glows beneath his words — to the Duchess, Lauresa. And most of all, his unrequited longing for his father's recognition.

"But enough of me, Mother," he says. "How have things been here? How is the new hand?"

She hired a new dairymaid to replace Lennis when he left: Liander, a capable girl just shy of sixteen winters. "Working well. Reeth and I miss your large hands and strong shoulders, but we've done without a man in the dairy for most of our lives." She puts an affectionate hand on his, to show she does indeed miss him very much.

And then she can delay telling him no longer. "Buttercup is gone."

He takes his hand away, puts it to his mouth, and she can see the tears spark in his hazel eyes. He's a farm boy — he's seen more death than most of his fellow recruits put together. But Buttercup was *his* bull. As a toddler he would sit on the placid beast's back and pretend to be a knight on a golden charger. As a lad, he showed his 'Budder' at fairs throughout the duchy under the more dignified mouthful of Little Water Tiffin's Golden Bud. He knows that most bulls are lucky to see half of Buttercup's years. But even Saoira, lifelong dairywoman, cries every time she puts down a cow or sends it to the butcher. And the tears she wept for Buttercup were multiplied by the years he'd been with her. She's glad her son still has a heart as soft as hers under his warrior's ribs. She moves around the table and encircles him with her arms for the second time that day, guiltily relishing the embrace despite the sadness of the moment.

"Why didn't you tell me?" he asked.

"I tried." She had started a letter three times, but could not find words that would not betray Lennis's identity. "When you sent word that you were coming home, I felt it would be easier to say in person."

"Did he suffer?"

She shakes her head. "He was comfortable, thanks to Radhan. But it was getting harder and harder for him to lie down or get up. I didn't want to wait till he could no longer stand." That was only partly true. She didn't want to wait for him to die naturally. Blood magic doesn't work with a corpse.

That is the part she can't bring herself to tell Lennis. It is safer, she reasons — for him, for her, and for Radhan — if he does not know.

Saoira owns horses now. The first she acquired was a sturdy roan gelding that pulls her dairy cart. So much easier than a hand-barrow for delivering cheese and milk. He matches her red-speckled cattle, and is not much finer or faster than they, with his sweet but plodding disposition. More recently, she bought a bay palfrey with an ambling gait to carry her up the mountains behind her herd. She is contemplating a third so that both she and Reeth can have their own mares. She has made Reeth a full partner in the increasingly prosperous dairy, and is looking forward to hiring more hands so the two of them can ride out when they have days of leisure.

Saoira is not a particularly good rider, but she's developing an eye for those who are. And for fine horseflesh. Which is why the first things she notices, as she is sweeping the stoop before opening, are the long legs and swinging stride of the grey mare coming up the road. The second is the perfect seat of the rider who pulls up in front of the creamery. The early autumn sun casts long shadows up the street and limns the rider's head in a gold and silver halo, leaving the woman's face in shadow.

"Saoira Little?" the rider asks, in a voice both musical and terrifying. She slides down from her horse without waiting for a reply. "May we talk inside?"

Saoira nods, suddenly cowed in the presence of this plain-dressed woman with the bearing of a queen and a horse fit for royalty. Saoira never felt so intimidated by Allenis, an actual duke, even at first glance.

"Please," she replies, and holds open the door to the creamery shop.

In the shop there is a small table, some stools, and no customers yet, but it still feels too public. She opens the door to the kitchen and shows the stranger through. Liander, the dairymaid, is making herself tea after feeding the livestock and mucking their pens.

"Can you mind the storefront for a bit, love?" Saoira asks, feeling guilty demanding even that much from the hardworking girl on her well-earned break.

Liander smiles. "Of course!" she says, bobbing her head to the guest as she leaves, teacup in hand. Lennis, agreeable as he is with everyone else, would have offered his mother a scowl and grumble before complying. As much as she misses him, Saoira acknowledges there are benefits to having staff that are not offspring.

"May I offer you something to drink …?" Saoira pauses, waiting for the stranger to introduce herself.

"Tea would be lovely," the still-unnamed woman replies.

"Please," Saoira says, motioning to the table with long benches on either side.

She turns her back to the unnerving stranger and busies herself with straining tea into a pair of mugs. She takes a small jug of fresh milk from the cold box and turns to put it on the table. When she sees what else has appeared there, the jug slips from her fingers and falls the last inch, splashing a single drop of creamy milk onto the worn wood. Saoira grasps the edge of the table, swaying, and falls to the bench with a thump that jolts her from hip to crown. Lennis's necklet rests on the table: tanned leather in the shape of a bull's head, its black eyes staring at her from amid the swirling gold patterns embossed upon it.

She tied it around her son's neck just half a year ago, as he sat at this table, his eyes still wet from learning of Buttercup's death. In that moment, she could swear she felt a tingle through her fingers, and she wasn't sure if she imagined the soft golden light that seemed to flow from the necklet and envelop Lennis. He didn't seem to notice it, but he turned to smile at her, his face more radiant than when he was a boy with his prize-winning bull at the fairground. Seeing the necklet here, without Lennis, takes the air from her body.

The stranger reaches out and puts a hand on Saoira's. "I apologize. Your son is well. I should have told you that first."

Saoira's heart is still rabbiting in her chest, and the gradually realized relief of the woman's words sets her hands shaking. "Yes, you should have," she replies, as anger replaces terror. She snatches the necklet and holds it in a fist that she presses to her mouth.

"He gave it to me. Willingly," the woman says.

Saoira's anger is at full boil. "He swore he'd never remove it. Not even to sleep."

"That is the problem with sons. They make promises they can't keep." The woman tips her head and gives a half smile. "I can be very persuasive."

Of the latter, Saoira has no doubt. The woman has somehow convinced Saoira to invite her into the kitchen without so much as an introduction.

"Lennis has been in the Duke's service, what, a year and a half now?" It isn't really a question. "And in all that time," the woman continues, "Andreg has not noticed a young man in his service with your eyes and his smile. The Duke has never been perspicacious ... but then, he doesn't have the benefit of something like that." She waggles a finger in the direction of the necklet, still clutched in Saoira's fist. "Leisanmira craftsmanship, but steeped in blood magic. Where did you get it?"

Saoira offers the easiest part of the truth.

"I paid a travelling saddler to make it. I don't recall his name."

The woman waves her long-fingered hand. "I don't need his name. I recognize the work. Where did you get the leather?"

When Saoira fails to answer through the fear clogging her throat, the woman lets out a long sigh. "Don't worry, I'm not with the College. Or the Mageguard. I have an abiding love for Woodkin, and I won't ask you to betray the name of the tree-priest who used blood magic to tailor this powerful protection for your son into the hide of an animal. For she must have worked with the craftsman to make the spell stick." Her light tone becomes serious, and she levels an ice-grey gaze at Saoira. "And I will no more betray my kinsman to the authorities than you would your tree-priest. In that much, and more, we have a mutual interest." The woman taps her fingers on the table a moment, as if thinking. "Let me tell you what I saw in a vision, midwinter last, and you tell me if I'm wrong. A woman of your height and build, leading slowly, so slowly, an aged bull into the woods. The snow is falling thick, hiding their tracks, and she carries no lamp—"

"Stop," says Saoira, unwilling to relive the memory under the spell of this woman's bewitching voice. "What is it you want? Yes, I sacrificed my bull to protect my son. Will you have me arrested? Or are you looking for gold to keep your silence?"

The woman laughs softly. "I have no need of your gold. I have need of your help."

Saoira's nerves are frayed, and she laughs in return: a sharp sound like the screech of a guinea hen. "What help can you possibly need from a farmer?"

"You sacrificed more than your bull for that spell. A yearling heifer, or a milk cow in her prime, would have had more vital magic to give. Your bull embodied many years of love from you both, which gave depth to the anima, but he was in his last days. A spell of protection for a son—that needed a mother's strength."

Saoira's hand, still clutching the necklet, steals to the left side of her chest, now hollow compared to the right. The scar has healed thanks to Radhan's skill and renewed powers. Not that Saoira needs either teat anymore, but she's grateful it was just the one.

The woman's gaze drops to the hand resting across Saoira's lopsided chest. "Your essence, as much as the bull's, is embedded in that ornament. It led me straight to your doorstep. And if I can follow it, so can others—who may have less sympathy for your son, and for you."

"You surely did not come all this way just to warn me of that."

The woman shakes her head. "No. I came as a kinswoman." Her half smile returns. "Surely you have suspected that you have Leisanmira blood in your veins?"

"None that I can prove."

"The proof is in this." The woman reaches over and gently unclasps Saoira's hands, peeling the necklet out. "There is power in you, if you chose to train it."

"I am happy with my dairy, my life here in Little Water."

"That's as may be. I hate seeing talent go to waste, though." There is a strange look in the woman's eyes, as if she's thinking of someone else. "Nonetheless, I'm not here to convince you to learn Leisanmira magic. This," she says, holding the necklet by its strings, "is too dangerous for Lennis to wear. There are Mageguard coming to Teillai, and it will be noticed."

Saoira feels as if her other breast has been ripped from her. All the sacrifices — the gold, Buttercup, her flesh, and the risks she, Radhan, and the young Leisanmira craftsman took — all in vain.

"But I am fond of him," the woman continues, "and I will do my best to see no harm comes to him."

"Who are you?" Saoira asks.

"A grandmother, a nurse, and a mother like you."

Saoira knows which family this grandmother belongs to. "And a practitioner of magic."

The woman tips her head in assent.

"And will you protect my child as much as your own?"

"As much as I can, without harm to my own." She lifts a hand to forestall protest. "It's as much as any mother can do." She stands, her gold-and-silver hair sparkling in the autumn light from the window. "But if you are willing to learn the magic that is your heritage, you can help me protect them all."

Saoira looks away from the plain-dressed yet dazzling stranger, who says she is not here to convince Saoira to learn magic. But she knows she is being manipulated, that the woman has used her persuasive voice and presence, equal to that of a trained actor, to stage this entire encounter, every beat and moment. Saoira still has the illusion of free will. She can turn the woman down, take her son's amulet, and give it back to him on his next return home — should he return. The woman has offered to protect him. Should she put her trust in the necklet she and Radhan paid so dearly to fashion, or in the stranger standing before her, whose quiet power seems to fill the room?

Amulets can be lost or stolen, and people can be fickle. Obligation weighs far more than gold. She did not turn down the Duke's gift of a golden calf, nor his gift of a son. Neither can she turn down this offer. She nods, and stands to look the woman eye to eye.

The stranger hands her back the amulet. Saoira ties it about her own neck, feeling the weight of magic settle on her shoulders.

§

For more high fantasy, family drama, and political intrigue set in the lands of the Ilmar, check out the spellbinding Allaigna's Song trilogy from JM Landels at Pulp Literature Press. https://pulpliterature.com/allaignas-song/

Now Available!

THE MAGICAL CONCLUSION TO THE MUST-READ EPIC TRILOGY

the adventures of Allaigna sing

simply a joy to read

keeps you turning pages from beginning to end

an immensely satisfying epic

PULPLITERATURE.COM/ALLAIGNAS-SONG/

OBJECTS AND BROKEN OBJECTS

DS Maolalai

DS Maolalai has received eleven nominations for Best of the Net and eight for the Pushcart Prize. His poetry has been released in three collections: Love is Breaking Plates in the Garden (Encircle Press, 2016), Sad Havoc Among the Birds (Turas Press, 2019), and Noble Rot (Turas Press, 2022).

Objects and Broken Objects

death comes to bodies
like a frightened trapped animal
lost within winter-dug
pits. and trying to get
out. and getting out
eventually. so what use the trap
when you collect it? it happens;
something bites through wire
and you decide to throw it away. I work
a job in maintenance. things go
beyond repair. objects
and broken objects. go on holiday
and forget the fridge is open. the motor burns—
milk floats
in your tea.

MOON EATER
EC Dorgan

EC Dorgan is a Métis writer from Alberta, Canada. She has stories published or forthcoming in Augur, The Dread Machine, and Metaphorosis. She has been known to go berry-picking. This story comes with a content warning for violence, murder, and grief . . . but also heartfelt beauty and courage.

Moon Eater

Sarah

I'm only pretending to play bingo. The game's in my blood, but I'm rusty. I spent days in these bingo halls as a child, sitting beside my grandma. It's my first time back in thirteen years. Now I have a degree and a research question. A university expense account. Training in field methods. A plan to find myself.

The first few games are a write-off; I'm missing half the caller's numbers. I'm not here to play, but it still irks me. By the second hour, I can almost keep up. I feel muscle memory awakening. Between games, my ears prick.

"I was berry picking … something in the bush …"

I scan the hall for the speaker, and then I see her—an old lady eating cheese twists at the back. She takes her time, choosing her words with care. I reach for my pen. Her companions roll their eyes. The old lady trails off.

I see her at the break at the snacks table. Come up beside her while she's pouring coffee. This time, I'm prepared. She puts down her styrofoam, and I'm there with the creamer. Our eyes meet, and I ask about the rougarou.

Elzéar

I'm looking out at the city from the skyscraper, trying to get through my client meetings, but the hunger's too much, rising from my haunches in waves. I take five for an Americano with an extra shot. Drink it fast and torch my tongue. My appetite's hotter.

Back in my office, I'm killing it. It's a cut-throat industry — my salary's based on sales. Me and my co-workers are badass — when we're not selling up clients, we're one-upping each other's extreme workouts and competing to see who can drink the most high-end whiskey at the bar.

But this new boss — she's not normal. She's hardcore on sales, then makes us sit in a circle and share. We're supposed to keep 'reflection journals'. I don't reflect. I have my own way of coping: I go home and put my headphone volume to the max. Get naked and howl at the shower head. Curl in a ball on the stained carpet and bite my thumbs until they bleed.

When the new boss convenes us, I press my pen into my blank pad and smash the nib. My co-workers complain about their lives and responsibilities. I would kill to be owned by the man, the job, the mortgage. I have the moon in my bones.

Sarah

Four days of spinning my wheels on Saskatchewan roads, getting weird looks in bingo halls, and I have only two pages to show for it. My notes aren't even good — more observations than actual research. I should be further ahead by now. I'm from here, I'm Métis. The university approved my topic: *Otipemisiwak (The People Who Own Themselves) and the Rougarou.* They're paying for my rental car. I came all the way here from Ontario.

I know this place. Spent time here when I was little, berry picking and playing bingo with my grandma, swimming in prairie lakes with my cousins. I thought I'd get more from that old lady at the bingo hall. But she clocked me right away as an outsider. Was it my clothes? And to think, she was a berry picker.

Berry picking — that's something special, the one thing that didn't come from a book. I can't come out and say it in my research plan, but it's couched there in my field methods. I learned about berry picking from my grandma.

You're more likely to meet a rougarou on a deserted road at night. They'll come after you if you're alone, or if you've been drinking, gambling, or playing cards — things that also mess with your memory or make you an 'unreliable witness'.

Berry picking, on the other hand — you have to be sharp. Don't want to run into a bear or an angry moose. You have to keep your wits, avoid getting lost. Sometimes, you find more than berries. My grandma thought berry picking was the world.

ELZÉAR

I start a damn journal. But it's a man's journal: black alligator leather with brushed metal edges. We sit in our circle, and I write about gouging clients and beating my record on pull-ups. I break three pens.

The moon swells. I lie in bed without sleeping. The bones in my hands and feet arch skyward, and my teeth pine for things to crunch. Spine itches, hungry to make ribs. There's vomit on my pillow in the morning. I can read the moon by it. Macaroni and undercooked steak when it's waxing. Eyeglasses, clothes tags, and acrylic nails when it wanes. The full moon is in three days — tomorrow will be worse.

It must be moon madness that makes me open that alligator leather over breakfast. I know I shouldn't, but once I start writing, I can't stop. I'm not writing about workouts anymore. Now, what I write makes me break prongs off my forks and crack the kitchen table with my grip. Things like her name ...

I arrive to work late, still wearing my headphones, serviette tucked in collar. My co-workers' eyes widen when they see me. I show them teeth and ramp up the volume. I take my journal and lock myself in my office. Look out the window and write.

S ARAH

Three days later, I've exhausted the bingo halls, and I can't take any more country markets with all their crocheted things and jams. I have to be back at the university on Monday. They're expecting a field study. I thought it would be easier, that people would still know me. All these years in the east, cut off from family ... I don't want to be a failure.

My grandma knew the old stories about rougarou, but I never asked her. I was too busy trying to leave, hungry to become someone else. I was seventeen when I moved east. I learned Métis folklore from books.

My grandma grew up around here. I remember the name of the community, but when I put it in my phone, I can't find it. I plug what I remember into my methodology: an old settlement based on river lots, links to the Resistance, those old Métis families. It meets all the indicators for my study.

I don't have a better idea, so I try it. Five minutes off the paved highway, my rental car GPS becomes a revolving circle. I know the general direction, maybe I can find it. My grandma didn't use maps. She navigated by land and bush, and especially by berries. She knew all the places for berries in this landscape.

The road is over-gravelled, so I have to drive slow. I pass sloughs and willows, and dust clouds rise from my wheels. The air is thick with dragonflies. There are no other cars. I have no idea where I am on the map, but I know I'm in saskatoon and chokecherry country — land for berry picking, land for rougarou.

Elzéar

Tonight's the full moon. Client meetings are intolerable. I've set my headphones to the max while I babble to some fool on a screen. Don't know what I'm saying. No idea who I'm meeting. I'm looking out the window at the city below. It's like any prairie city: there's a perfect line where the city stops, and the land opens up to sky.

I've had this view for years, but only now it hits me — it faces east. That's where my home is. My wife. That's where the moon took me.

When we gather for the reflection session, that journal's burning up in my hands. It's cursed, what it's doing to me, stirring up memories, feeding this crazy July moon. They say the Wolf Moon's in winter, but I know it's these long days and short nights that fuel the moon's rage.

I seethe in my suit while my co-workers reflect. I can't bear another moment in this skyscraper, this city. Another morning, waking to a nightmare on my pillow. I'm tired of shitting eyeglasses.

When my boss asks me to share, I put down my work phone and laptop. I rip off my lanyard and tell her, "I'm done."

I hold that journal so tight it scalds my knuckles. I take the elevator all thirty-two floors down, and step eastward into sun.

Sarah

The sky looms and looms. It's hard to see, with all the dragon-flies splattered on the windshield. The only sound for miles is crickets. The gravel thins. Now the road is mostly potholes. A coyote crosses in front of my car. I'm going to need gas soon.

My indicator light's flashing red, and I'm almost on empty, when I come to a town. It's not my grandma's, but it's close. There's a gas station with an old-fashioned pump. I have to ask the attendant how to use it. Something about her face nags at me.

I follow her to the cash and take my time rummaging for my wallet.

"Have you seen the rougarou?" The gravel's parched my throat. I stumble on the syllables.

Her lip twitches, but her slouch stills.

I change tack and ask if she knows my grandma's town.

Her face changes. "Who's your grandma?"

I should have known—we're related. It's a risk in these parts— all these big Métis families. She declares us third cousins.

"You should meet my Uncle Joe."

She tells me he knows old stories. He's not on the map either, so she sends me off with directions. His dogs find me before I reach his house. I follow tire tracks through long grass, to what might have been a farm. Rocks and twigs crunch under the chassis, and I hope the rental company won't ding me.

When I park the car, the dogs mob me, leaving slobber on my jeans, then run back to the road after a distant car. An old man in a walker shuffles to the screen door. I have no idea what time it is.

"Florence's granddaughter?"

My third cousin told him about me. We sit in his kitchen, and I make him tea.

"A big one, I saw." He points to the road. "That rougarou, it almost got me."

I pull out my notebook. He says it's from grandma's community. She even met it once. He touches his suspenders when he speaks. My grandpa wore suspenders.

I want to ask more, but Uncle Joe changes the subject. He asks about my relatives. I shake my head. We were closer before I moved.

"Florence, she loved picking berries."

I shouldn't digress, but I put down my pen to listen.

"She picked berries all around here. She knew the best patches. Them saskatoons, chokecherries."

I can taste them. We'd be driving on the highway, and my grandma would say, "Here." My grandpa would park his hatchback and put down his seat for a nap, while I'd follow my grandma into the bush.

Uncle Joe asks about my cousins. I have nothing to say. I search in my notebook for the question to bring us back.

He invites me to stay for dinner—my third cousin and some other relatives are coming. I almost consider it. What it would be to see them. But how would I explain myself after so long away? I make an excuse. He tells me I'm always welcome. The dogs chase me out.

Elzéar

I'm in a daze till I hit the refineries on the eastern edge of the city. There's a new scratch on the windshield. Could be the music; it's loud enough. But I'm wearing headphones, so it must be the moon.

Past the refineries, my ethmoid starts to rattle. There's a bump on the road, and the bone elongates. It twists without warning, and I come up fast behind a hatchback. Barely brake to avoid rear-ending it. I flash my lights and open my window. I throw a pop can at the car but miss.

I drive on. My mind is half dog. I might not have my wallet. No idea what happened to my phone. That journal burns on the passenger seat. Memories roar when I look at it. Sweat is dripping off the steering wheel. My curling fingers can't start the AC.

By the time the sun sets, I'm in Saskatchewan, long off paved highway. This is the landscape I know, where open prairie turns to willow bushes and poplar bluffs and, farther north, spruce. I can smell the South Saskatchewan winding nearby. There's good hunting in this bush. I had traplines in these trees. This wasn't Saskatchewan when I lived here.

My headphones are deafening, but the crickets are louder. I left the road some time ago. Grass and bush tangle under my car. I taste the night with the roof of my mouth. There's river, bush, and something older. Close my eyes, and I feel it coming up through the gas and steering wheel. I'm not far now.

Sarah

I eat dinner in my room — cold pizza from the nearby gas station. It leaves a layer of grease on my teeth. I'd eat better at Uncle Joe's. But the thought of the questions … Would my relatives still know me? They don't even know I'm back.

Growing up, we were close. I can't think of a childhood memory without them. Even when I moved away, they were always calling, asking after me, inviting me home to visit. I was too busy with my studies, and my new life in the east. After a while, they stopped calling. All those years in Ontario — I worked, I studied, but I never belonged. I don't know what happened to me. Sometimes, I think my research is less about Métis folklore and more about finding my way home.

Elzéar

I leave the car by the river. It's faster on these feet. They know this land, they curve to the shape of it. Sometimes I'm on road, sometimes I'm walking through bush or staggering through sloughs. I'm leaning on willows and breathing in night. The moon is getting brighter.

There's a clap that's not thunder, and the world cracks in two. Something in my skull bursts, and my vision turns grey. The curve of my spine snaps straight, and my new ribs reach for the sky. My whole body shudders, then my head whips back, and the moon pulls me up like a hook. I'm a moment suspended. Then my knees change their bend, and I fall.

I lift my head and howl into the night. My jaws open and open, and I eat the alligator-skin journal in a single bite. I open my mouth wider, this time for the moon — but it's too big to eat.

The bush is thick with things to stalk, and I'm moon-hungry, famished. But even now, something else pulls at me: that damn journal, burning a hole in my gut. This is where I made a home, this is where I had a family.

I went out only once, under that angry July moon. They said not to go alone — I should have listened. This is where I was damned. I still remember our horse, lying gutless in the morning. Pitou, that yapper, missing. I never did find the cow … My gut was so heavy I couldn't dress. And the pain — I passed horse teeth and a terrier jaw that evening.

SARAH

My phone buzzes. It's an invitation from the university to present my findings on Monday morning. I stare at the date. Can't understand how this week has sped by. I thought it would be easier, that this land would take me back. I feel like a stranger. I'll never be a real scholar. Would my family take me back? Or have they disowned me too? I don't even own myself anymore.

I stare at the pizza box. The motel room's thick with the stench of congealed grease. It's suddenly unbearable. I need air.

When I step outside, the moon takes my breath. All these years in the closed-in city—it's like I'm seeing it for the first time. Didn't even realize it was the full moon. And I should know. I've read the literature.

I get a thought. I scroll to maps, and my grandma's town is showing again. This time, it's closer. GPS is a crapshoot around here, I'd have just as much luck on foot. Could try navigating by berry and bush. Maybe I can salvage something, get some notes out of it.

It feels good to be outside after all these days in the car. The sky's even bigger at night. And that moon ... Each time I look, it gets me. There are fewer mosquitoes on the road. Dust and gravel wedge in my toes and make my flip-flops slide.

The night helps me think. It gives me perspective. It's not the end of the world if I don't complete this field study. I can revert to the literature. Spend a week at the library. I'll survive.

By the time I stop for my bearings, I've lost track of time. The gas station is somewhere behind me. The motel is farther back, I barely see it. Can't believe I've come this far. I should go back.

The sky's so bright it could be day. I still hear crickets. I scan the landscape. My grandma would say this is berry country. I breathe it in. So many memories in the bush with her. I shouldn't have left.

I blink and I see it. A big dog—no, a rougarou. All this time studying, and still I'm not ready for it. I blink again, and it's still there, in the middle of the road, straightening—no, turning toward me. My breath catches. I lose a flip-flop. I never believed the stories, but now … I don't like what my heart is doing.

The beast shifts. Something rises from my stomach. I've read too many sources. I search for my shoe. My heart is wild. I try to summon the literature, but nothing comes. It sniffs the air. My knees falter—I catch myself. It turns its head. Please don't let it see me.

Elzéar

My baby boy loved that terrier. Everything that dog did made him laugh. My boy was my world. I can still see him, gurgling and clapping. I smell the air—it's baby skin. Those crickets—they're my wife's laugh. They're all around me. I look up at the moon. It's nothing next to my wife. My baby boy laughs, he makes the moon small. We were family.

The landscape bows to them. Sticks on the road are my wife's comb. A dead rabbit for the fur-lined boots she made our boy. He grew out of them fast, so I trapped another rabbit, and she made another pair. He didn't grow out of those.

Now, the memories won't stop. These are different memories, these are unspeakable memories. They're tiny fingers and tiny feet, the tiny toys and tiny boots.

I howl, but my voice cracks. I bite my thumb, but it doesn't bleed. The moon ignores me. Shame is bigger than everything.

SARAH

I blink again. It doesn't look so much like a dog now. More like a man, prostrate on the road. My heart hasn't slowed. Legs still shaking.

The man, or animal, lifts his head. It doesn't move, but now I'm certain it sees me. It sniffs the air. The literature can't help me now. The gas station must be five hundred metres away. The rougarou's closer.

I head for the gas station, and it follows, steady, behind me. I try to go faster, but my flip-flops slip from my feet. I am getting blisters. I should have asked Uncle Joe how he got away. I reach for my notebook, but I must have dropped it. I look back and shudder—the monster's closer. I can barely keep my pace, and I'm getting out of breath. I look to the land. Panic rises. I try to distract myself.

I picked berries with my grandma in places like this. We'd bring back our pails, tired and happy, and climb back into my grandpa's hatchback. He'd adjust his hat, and we'd go bringing berries to relatives. Sometimes, on the way, we'd stop for bingo. My grandma owned herself.

Something in the moonlight catches my eye. I stop. It might be saskatoons. Or chokecherries. I can't see from the road, but somehow I feel it, must be muscle memory. The gas station isn't so far now. The monster's not slowing, but if I walk fast, I might reach it. I look back at those berries and think of my grandma.

ELZÉAR

Something rustles in the bush. I stop and sniff. It might be prey. I hesitate then step off the gravel. I've always been a good tracker. My footsteps are soft on the long grass. I smell fear. I let the scent lead me.

She surprises me when she steps out from the bush. That woman from the road. She's wearing flip-flops, impractical. Does she not know the dangers? There are monsters that roam under that angry July moon, monsters like me . . .

She doesn't move, but something glistens in her hand. I sniff. Her smell is different. I step forward. She opens her palm—it's the moon.

I blink, and she eats it. She reaches into the bush and takes another. The Wolf Moon is nothing compared to it. Our eyes meet. She doesn't look like prey.

I turn away. A memory awakens. Her face reminds me. Another time, this same bush. Those same eyes. I tracked the woman all the way from the hatchback. Thought she was easy prey. But when she opened her hands—the whole world was in there. I still cower when I think of it.

The light of the gas station shines back at me. Somewhere beyond, I've abandoned my car. I could drive to the city, or build a den in it. Tomorrow, I'll shit paper and black alligator leather, but in this moment, I own myself. The thought's too much. I try to howl, but can only whine.

TO MAKE YOU STAY

Purbasha Roy

Purbasha Roy *is a writer from Jharkhand, India. Her work has appeared or is forthcoming in SIAMB, Bluestem, DASH, View, The Bayou Review, long con magazine, Hive Avenue, and elsewhere.*

To make you stay

To make you stay I toy you with after images of
remains. I alone shall sit on couch and wait for you
to catch up and feed me, a fresh baked sonnet. Wind
understanding the absence would try compensate &
dance among grass flowers. If this happening had any
feasible sound, what would that be, but the sounds of
becoming an estuary. I don't know, how many have
experienced hunger is not a journey from a hole to
another. It is a conflict within. In defence of balances,
kitchen would search for pepper smells. I avoid. If you
leave how my sneezes would stiffen like silence of
blank paper. Vaporize of words from atmosphere of
sheets. Like *Sanskrit* from Indian streets. For you won't
be around, outcome of conversations with reflections and
shadows would be brain splitting, between *missing &*
coping. On thinking of building a bridge between skies
and earth I could only discover *rain.* So, what would
that mean if you and me at a greater distance shall
inflorescence me inside the concert of all things falling

NOBODY KNOWS IT BUT ME

Franco Amati

Nobody Knows It but Me

Back when I had a brain that worked, I only ever said nice things. I would think different things, of course — things that weren't nice. But I only ever let the nice things come out, because I wanted to seem like a good person. Ever the peacemaker. If you can't say something nice, don't say anything at all. Now I really can't say anything at all, and it kills me.

"What would you like for lunch, Ellis? Chicken salad or tuna? Maybe some rice?" Martha asked. She held up my special menu displaying huge, high-definition photos of various food options.

Cheeseburger. I want a cheeseburger.

"I think he glanced at the chicken salad. Get the chicken salad, Cindy. Ellis wants my chicken salad."

"He does not," Cindy said. "He's just staring off into space."

"Get the Decider," Martha said. "I showed you how to hook it up. You grab the sensors right there, and, yeah, that's it. Right on the temple. One on each side — yep."

"Do I press this button here?" Cindy asked. At least Cindy smelled nice. And she wasn't as dense as the rest of the workers. "Like this, Martha?"

Martha was older, meaner, a little controlling. She was the manager at Heraldry House, and she enjoyed letting everyone know it. "Right, and then you make eye contact with him and clearly ask the question out loud … and wait …"

"Wait for what?"

"You wait for the answer. Jesus, don't be stupid. The machine interprets his brain signals, and the auto-voice thingy tells you what he wants. But you have to give him the choices again or it doesn't work."

Cindy sighed, held up the menu, and bit her lower lip. I could feel her trying to find the answer in my face. But all I did was fixate on her deep brown eyes. I focused intently on nothing but those brown eyes. Cleared my mind of everything except cheeseburgers and brown eyes.

"Aye-want-chick-en-sal-ed," the Decider said in its wonderful tinny voice, a voice that only I seemed to understand wasn't my own.

All day long, I was surrounded by staff who got paid to take care of me, who believed they were well-trained in interpreting my grunts and sighs, my blinks and finger flicks. I don't really know any of these people. I don't like any of these people. They think caring for me means holding my hand and gently running their fingers through my hair, as if that superficial physical contact is what I need to remind me that I'm still inhabiting a body.

I wish I could tell them to leave me alone — to put the food in front of me and get out of the way.

"Aye-want-chick-en-sal-ed," the Decider repeated.

"Chicken salad. See. Told you he glanced at it. He likes my chicken salad. Don't you, Ellis, dear?"

No. I hate your fucking chicken salad. And I hate you.

Martha placed her big, clammy hand on my hand and squeezed my fingers. So obnoxious, this woman.

The genius who invented that Decider is probably set for life. I bet he congratulates himself every morning for all the disabled people he thinks he's helping with his machine. But I'll tell you what — it doesn't interpret raw thoughts. It doesn't reveal what I really feel or want. Not at all.

Maybe it interprets something fuzzy, you know, some distorted signal, something filtered through the expectations of others, of society — I don't know. Maybe it keys in on that socially acceptable thing — what the average, polite civilian would say in a normal situation.

I guess they don't realize I'm not civilized anymore. I no longer operate in the real world. Ellis wants a goddamn cheeseburger, and he wants to eat it in a quiet room by himself. Is that too much to ask?

"Mmm, isn't that good? That's it, Ellis. You love that zesty mayo!"

Fuck you, Martha. I chewed up her blobs of goop. The slight crunch of the occasional piece of celery livened things up. I got the notion to spit some of it back up on her hand just to piss her off — and that way Cindy might feed me the rest — but I didn't.

"Hey, Cindy. Once I'm done here, you go ahead and get him ready for bed. It's nearly seven, and I can tell he's tired."

I'm not tired, Martha. Just tired of you.

She shoved a sleeping pill into my mouth and smushed it down on my tongue. Then, with her crusty-ass fingers, she forced my mouth closed. "Ah, swallow ... yes, swallow," she said in a hushed voice like she was talking to a damn baby.

God forbid they leave me by myself. I have absolutely zero desire to eat food with other humans. Never have. There is only one person I remember enjoying meals with. Roxanna. *Oh, Roxanna. Where are you?* She could be dead now for all I know — it's not like they let me use the internet in here. All I know is that she said goodbye to me in the hospital one day, a day I barely remember because I was still recovering and high on some kind of drug. I never saw her again.

Something happened to me. They told me it was an accident. But no one talks to me like I'm an adult. No one's given me the whole story. I'm mostly locked in my body now — head's pretty messed up, and my limbs have atrophied.

I just wish I could find out what happened to *her.* No one ever mentioned her again. Maybe I made her up. Maybe she never existed at all. The mystery consumes me, haunts me. And there's no device that can reveal to my caretakers the depths of my desire to know what happened to Roxanna.

Imagine if the only person you ever cared about disappeared, and you were stuck with a bunch of randos doing things for you all day long. A revolving door of helpers who got paid just a shade over minimum wage to pretend they liked you.

They will never know me. No one will ever know me again.

Martha clocked out. I could hear her shitty Corolla sputtering its way out of the garage. I was left with Cindy for the rest of the night. Cindy's gotta be in her early thirties. I think that was about Roxanna's age when I last saw her. "Hey, Ellis. Want to try something different tonight before bed?" Cindy asked.

I had already closed my eyes, hoping she'd think I'd fallen asleep.

She began to read. Then I felt a flutter in my stomach. Somehow, a wave of . . . something . . . hit me right in the gut, and no, this time it wasn't nausea from the chicken salad. It was nostalgia. The line she was reading was from my favourite book, a novel that had been collecting dust on my shelf ever since I arrived at Heraldry House.

There's no way Cindy could have known how much I loved this book. I listened to the prose spoken in her soft, gentle, bedtime voice. Yeah, Cindy definitely wasn't as dense as the rest. That night I decided that Cindy was better than all the other workers at Heraldry House combined.

She stopped after an hour or so. It seemed she had dozed off. The book rested near my hand, so close I could almost turn the page myself. I wanted more. I needed more. Emotion blazed in me, as if something crucial waited just beyond the next page.

I mustered all my strength, all my intention, and attempted to turn the page myself. But, instead, with an awkward flick of my index finger, the book slid off the bed and landed on the hardwood floor. The noise startled Cindy awake.

She bent to retrieve the book. "What's this?" she said, inspecting the inside cover. "Some kind of note?"

When the Decider Plus finally came out, it felt like a major breakthrough. The new version allowed for open-ended responses. I was no longer limited to multiple-choice conversation.

One of the first things Cindy asked me when they tested out the Decider Plus was, "So, Ellis … what do you want?"

"Roxanna," I said with crisp, absolute certainty. Even the voice that came out of the device was more assertive. Less mechanical, less feeble. It was still a vague approximation of my actual voice, but, hey, it was something.

"Did Roxanna write the note inside your book?"

"Yes, Roxanna."

I couldn't say much, but we were at least approaching a semblance of dialogue.

"What should we do today, Ellis?"

"Find Roxanna."

When Cindy had discovered the note in the back of the book, it seemed to ignite some curiosity in her, and this response lit another spark. I think she had ideas now — plans about how she could really help me. "Okay," she said, nodding up and down, determined. "I'll see what I can do."

Cindy volunteered to accompany me to my next medical check-up. Normally it was Martha who drove the van and took the residents to their appointments. "*You* want to take him? But I thought you didn't like driving?" Martha said.

Cindy grabbed the keys and twirled them around her finger. "Guess I'm getting a little tired of doing all the laundry," she said.

Martha shrugged. "Fine, by all means. Just make sure he's back by dinner. Oh, and maybe take him for a stroll through the park too. My Ellis loves the ducks!"

Ugh, this woman with the fucking ducks.

At the doctor's, they did the usual. MRI, physical exam, and the standard battery of cognitive tests.

"I think he's a lot happier now," Cindy said to the doctor. "Open-ended responses are a miracle. He's a lot easier to work with now that we can communicate better."

"That's good. He's still struggling with his recall. The cortical damage was severe. But people have a way of bouncing back. Best to keep his mind as active as possible."

"He loves when I read to him. Right, Ellis?" she said, smiling.

It was strange. Cindy seemed more empowered than I'd ever seen her. It was as if the prospect of my improvement motivated her. Who would have thought? They'd finally found a caretaker who actually cared about her job.

"He keeps mentioning this name, though. Roxanna. Is this someone we should know about? He never gets visitors. I know next to nothing about him. Not too sure about his family either. Was he ever married?"

The doctor looked through my file, taking longer than expected to give an answer. "No, I don't see any record of a spouse. I'm afraid I'm not able to tell you anything more than that." She shut the folder. "Maybe it's a character from a book. Or a name from a song? Could be anything, dear. We can translate the neural signals into words, but what the words really represent — that's anyone's guess," she said with a shrug.

Back in the car, Cindy vented her frustration. "These doctors are no help. Don't worry, we'll find your Roxanna."

On the front passenger seat was the Manila folder containing my medical file. I couldn't believe she swiped it from the nurse's station.

"Her name is Roxanna DeSantis. And for some reason, she was listed as your emergency contact when you were admitted, but then everything was crossed out. They redacted her information. Who are you, Roxanna? And what did you do?" she said, not so much to me, but in a sort of suspicious, rhetorical tone.

We stopped at the library. She did a search for Roxanna DeSantis. She positioned my wheelchair next to her in front of the screen, and I tried to keep up with her rapid scrolling. Images, text, profiles — a cascade of visual information, data that all seemed more confusing than helpful. I could barely keep track.

None of the photographs jogged my memory. Cindy read through various news articles and social media posts. I couldn't remember what the hell Roxanna even looked like. But I had this deep intuition that if I heard her voice again I might recognize her.

I started to worry that even if we found her, it wouldn't matter. None of what she and I had before — if we had anything at all — would hold much weight now. I mean, look at me. I can't do anything. Why would someone who loves you just disappear?

"I think we got the information we need. I'm pretty sure your Roxanna lives on the North Shore of Long Island. And she works right here." She held up a printed page and pointed with her finger. "See that big glass building? That's where we're gonna get the answers you deserve."

It always seemed to me that people had more to say than they actually said. It felt like Cindy knew more than she was letting on — but maybe I was just projecting. Anyway, I'd seen a lot of medical facilities, and that glass building definitely had the look of a substantial type of hospital.

"Do you remember Long Island?" she asked. "You lived there for a while, apparently. This is a state research hospital. Does it look familiar?"

"Not familiar," I said.

Though I didn't remember living on Long Island, I did recall a beach in that hazy way you remember moments from childhood. Sometimes I dream about the shore, about my toes in the sand, the salt water in my eyes. But it's just a beach. It could be any beach. Long Island didn't mean anything specific to me.

"We just have to find a way to get there. Maybe we can convince Martha to get approval for a trip. I think there's an aquarium there. That's educational, right? Heraldry House might approve it for, like, a weekend or something. Don't worry, Ellis. I'm going to help you find her."

I still didn't know why it mattered so much to her. Why was Cindy helping me? Did I really matter that much to her? So much that she'd go through all this bullshit for me?

The clock on the wall said 6:45. It was getting dark out. I can't remember the last time I was out of the house this late. *Martha's gonna fucking yell at you, Cindy. She's gonna be so pissed off we're late for dinner, her face is gonna blow up like a big raspberry. Better brace yourself, Cindy.*

"Here, have some juice. I don't think you had anything to drink today." She punctured the hole of a juice box and some purple liquid squirted out. "Take a sip," she said. I sucked out as much juice as I could. Then she put the straw to her own mouth, crushed the box with her fist, and sucked out the remaining liquid inside. "Ahhh," she sighed. "Come on, it's late. We gotta go."

We arrived back to find Heraldry House in a tizzy. Martha was steaming. "Dinner is cold!" she said. "Where have you been?"

"We were at the park and lost track of time," Cindy said.

"At the park, huh?"

"You know how he loves the ducks," Cindy said, out of breath and avoiding direct eye contact with the boss lady.

Martha had set the table. Napkins were folded. She had portioned out each serving. My tomato soup had already developed that gross, oily film on top.

"Get him washed up. If he doesn't eat in the next twenty minutes, his whole medication schedule will be off." Martha threw her hands up in the air. "Then he'll be late to bed. His whole routine will be out of whack, and we'll have to deal with the mood swings."

Mood swings? Routine? I didn't know what this bitch was talking about. *Lay off, woman.*

Martha tore the keys from Cindy's hand. "Now, go!"

Cindy took a step back, wary.

Shit. She was going to check the car's mileage. Martha always kept track for reimbursement. She'd figure out we went farther out than the park.

"Wait, Martha!" Cindy shouted, but she couldn't leave me by myself. She ran to the window. "Fuck! The folder. Your files."

We're screwed. So much for finding Roxanna …

Cindy sighed, shook her head. "Come on. You're probably starving. There's nothing we can do at this point. Maybe Martha will understand."

Cindy was drying my face when I heard the living room door slam. Detective Martha had figured it out. The jig was up.

"Cindy! What is this? No, don't tell me. I *know* what this is. The question is, why do you have it?"

Cindy just stood there, helpless.

"No explanation?" Martha put one hand on her hip and waved the folder in the air with the other. "I have to turn you in. Simple as that. They're going to fire you, Cindy — unless you have some reasonable explanation for why you have Ellis's confidential file."

"Do you know about Roxanna?"

"We are not having this discussion. Gather your things. Your shift is up. I'll phone you in the morning."

Cindy stormed out. That was it for the night. Martha fed me my dinner, shoved my sleeping pills down my throat, and put me to bed.

The next morning I was awakened not by Cindy, but by a totally new worker. For days, not a word was uttered about what had happened to Cindy, but a week later I overheard a conversation between two of the new employees. She'd been transferred to another house.

I have this dream. Well, maybe it's more like a vision or fantasy. Often it comes during the day, but I don't really know for sure. There's little difference between day and night, waking and sleep, for me at this point. But it is a scene of . . . intimacy. I am in a calm, quiet apartment. The lighting is dim and reassuring. It is *my* apartment. I live alone, in peace. I am independent, functional, doing purposeful things. Using my own imagination to act on the world and to change my environment by my own will. I feel strong.

There's always this one person there. Her face — I have a rough idea of it — is familiar, but it changes every time. She looks at me with adoration. I know she sees my fire, my strength. She doesn't see me as some *thing* that needs help. She leaps into my arms and squeezes me tight, knowing I won't break. I carry her inside, and on the sofa she straddles me, clings to me, like she will never let me go.

One afternoon, I was snapped out of this daydream by a familiar voice. "We're getting out of here. We're going to find Roxanna."

Cindy had returned. She explained that staffing shortages allowed her to cover for a sick night-shift worker. "They were desperate. Of course I wasn't too thrilled to see Martha again," she whispered, "but now we have our chance."

Cindy grabbed my things and wheeled me out. In the living room, I noticed Martha slumped on the couch, asleep. "I borrowed a few of your sleeping pills. Crushed them up into her coffee. Hope you don't mind."

I laughed hard on the inside.

In the car, she strapped me in. "We probably have about four or five hours before Martha wakes up and reports us missing. By then we'll already be crossing the bridge to Long Island." Cindy buckled her seatbelt and started the engine. "I hope you know I am totally getting fired for this."

We arrived in some small beach town on the North Shore. The sun was going down, and the salty ocean breeze felt cool on my face.

The beach house appeared to be empty. Cindy looked around the property for signs of life. I was enthralled by the sights and sounds and smells of the beach. It all felt familiar, but in a strange way, like a childhood home.

A man emerged from a neighbouring house and asked what we were doing. Cindy explained, and asked about the residence. "Does a woman named Roxanna live here?"

He scratched a tuft of white hair on his head. "I think that was the woman's name. A guy and a girl lived there, actually — a while back. Nice couple, if my mind serves me right."

"Any idea where they went? Where she went?"

"Heard they moved. I think she used to work over at the university. Maybe a student over at Stony Brook, not too far from here. There's a big research hospital. You can spot it from the parkway. Biggest building on the North Shore — modern, all glass, got these weird boxy structures all around it."

"We have to find somewhere to stay," Cindy said to me. "With any luck, if she's still there, we can meet her in the morning."

I felt this urge to be near the water, so I began moving my arms around to get Cindy's attention.

"What's wrong, Ellis? What is it you want?"

"Water," the Decider Plus said for me.

"I have a bottle in the car."

"No, *water*," I repeated, concentrating on the surf. "Ocean."

"It's beautiful, isn't it?" Cindy said. "Sir, is it all right if I leave his things here for a bit?"

"Of course. I'll be on my deck. I'll keep an eye out. Young man seems to like the beach," he said. "Sunset's gorgeous tonight."

Cindy took a deep breath and lifted me up with all her strength. It felt strange, her carrying me. She lugged me about fifty yards to where the sand met the water.

She took off my shoes and socks and removed her own as well. She supported my weight with an arm around my back, allowing me to lean on her as the tide came in and rolled out. We sat quietly and watched the sun go down. The horizon was streaked with rich pinks and oranges across a brilliant backdrop of evening blue.

My feet looked so scrawny next to hers.

"I was always tall," she said. "Kids at school used to make fun of my feet. Then I got into basketball and finally embraced my size. Played three years in college. Decided to roll the dice in the draft. Then I got injured, and that was it." She got quiet, letting the information set in.

It was the most I had learned about her life. Unlike Martha, Cindy wasn't the type of person to talk much about herself. I noted the long scar on her leg; her jeans were rolled up above her knees.

"The guy I was dating played too," she continued. "He got a contract to play in Europe. He was supposed to pick me up one afternoon from a PT session, but instead I got a text from him saying he was leaving on a plane the next morning."

I felt her sorrow, her loneliness. It all began to make sense—why she cared, why she wanted to help someone like me. She was as abandoned as I was.

How long do sunsets take? Could we just sit here until the stars come out? I closed my eyes and stayed in that moment with her as long as I could.

A flood ruptures my eardrums, my eyes burn, my mouth fills with water and salt. Waves crash. My heart is ablaze with panic and terror. My screams do nothing. I am pulled down, deeper into darkness. A hand reaches out. I am saved ... brought ashore. Lips meet mine. Air fills my lungs. I expel brackish foam. The angel has brought me back to life.

I was in a hospital. I sat in some kind of tube, a huge, humming machine. My thoughts poured from my mind, glided eloquently off my tongue, and shot themselves into the air. *Wow.* I had forgotten what it felt like for my thoughts to map directly onto words. Forgotten how to speak. "Where the hell is Cindy?" I asked.

"She's gone into custody," the doctor said "She turned herself in. Don't worry. The officers said she was cooperative on the condition that we be as transparent with you as possible about ... everything. She told us you're ready to hear it, and that it's better for you—well, for you moving forward, anyway—to under-stand what happened before you arrived at Heraldry House."

The sad-looking woman next to him nodded. "And we agree with her, Ellis. You should know the truth."

"What is this place? What is this fucking thing? Get me out of here!" I was strapped in, surrounded by glass, while an awful droning noise filled the tube. I breathed in cool, vaporous air.

"It's called the Conduit. Our scientists and engineers are still working on it," the man said as he scribbled down notes in a small pad of paper. "I'm told you've been doing well, communicating via Decider technology. This is the successor to the Decider Plus: the next leap in human-machine interface technology. Soon they'll be in hospitals and rehabilitation centres all over the country."

I noted the woman's name tag. *Dr DeSantis.* "Are you ... Roxanna?"

She put her head down, closed her eyes briefly. "I'm not who you think I am," she said.

"Ellis," the man continued, "you were a participant in our early pilot studies for the first iteration of the Decider. I'm not sure how else to tell you this. About five years ago, my wife, Roxanna—she was in med school at the time—was walking home one evening, and—"

She cut him off mid-sentence. "I saved you. You were drown-ing, and I saved you. I thought I recognized you from campus. You were a graduate student in the philosophy department. Anyway, I dove in, did CPR. We don't know for sure, but the therapists believed you were trying to—" She paused. "Anyway, that doesn't matter. We tried to contact your family, but no one was willing to visit."

"We don't know for sure what you were doing in the water that night," the male doctor said. "It was late, and you were by yourself. As a result of being underwater for so long, you suffered severe brain damage due to lack of oxygen."

"But … the book. Roxanna, your note in the back of my book."

"I gave that to you as a parting gift after your hospital stay. Everyone, including Dr Stern here, agreed the best thing was for you to be transferred to a residential home. They felt you were becoming too attached to me. I looked after you during your recovery. We had lunches together. I read stories to you. I wanted to see you through, help you get better—get you the help you needed."

"Roxanna suggested to my team that you take part in our trial," Dr Stern said. "I heard you're doing much better—that the Decider Plus is really helping."

My mind raced. It was too much to take in. Something had happened—I'd tried to off myself, or I'd had an accident, or … I had thought my life before was so much better. I thought I had lost so much. But, really … what did I lose? The real Roxanna wasn't the person my mind had conjured her up to be. She wasn't in love with me. In fact, no one loved me. I needed … I needed … I needed to rest.

"Thank you both for helping me," I said. But I was no longer enjoying the sensation of lucid speech. "I'd like to go back now."

"Before you go," Dr Stern said, "now that you're communicating more effectively with the Decider Plus, I'm going to recommend you early access to the Conduit as soon as it's available in your area. The neural translation accuracy is phenomenal, and you'll be able to have full conversations and work through things with other people."

For a moment, I made direct eye contact with Roxanna. But it hurt, and I said nothing.

"It was good to see you, Ellis," Roxanna said. "Everything *will* get better."

I didn't believe the doctors when they said things would get better. But, in time, they did. The months went by, and helpers continued to come and go. Martha got promoted, and I didn't have to deal with her anymore.

Cindy was dismissed from Heraldry House, but we'd both expected that. Thanks to my testimony, she didn't get in too much legal trouble. After a while, she got a better job, and things started looking up for her as well. The Conduit Portable works wonders for me, and we talk all the time.

My body is still limited, but my voice is now free.

I am in my own space. I speak my own words, and I change the world. There is a knock at the door, and it is the person I love, the one I am promised to. I open the door with my voice, and she, my angel, enters. We glide to the bed, lighter than air. We are one, in all times, all moments, joined in consciousness, free to do as we please, always.

ALL THE RAGE

Aaron Poochigian

Aaron Poochigian, *award-winning author of four books of poetry, has published in* Best American Poetry, The Paris Review *and* POETRY. *Before this excerpt from his verse-novel* Mr. Either/Or: All the Rage *(June 2 0 2 3), 'you', an FBI agent, have just offed Aquila Blair, an enemy agent who threatened your girlfriend Li-Ling Levine. Li-Ling has just discovered that she is carrying your child.*

Find Mr. Either/Or: All the Rage *here: www.amazon.com/ Mr-Either-Rage-Aaron-Poochigian/dp/B0B5KQVCPV*

One Plus One Is Three

You can relax now, killer. You have rolled
the monster's corpse up in the blood-stained rug
and dumped the whole burrito in a cold
puddle behind Armando's Midtown Deli.
It could be weeks before the thing gets found.

Yes, you have done your chores and now are snug
in bed and fondling Li-Ling's little belly,
imagining the kid inside of her
in black and white, like in an ultrasound.

(The 'we' you are has now increased to three.)

Mostly asleep, you mumble,
                              "If I were
to get a ring, what size should it, like, be?"

"Was that, like, a proposal?"
                              "Yeah, I guess."

She laughs, then answers you: a cosmic "Yes."

(Afterward, though, in an exhausted silence
all the nasty things you have to do
for work descend on her. She lies there seeing
criminal menaces, vile acts of violence.
How could she not half regret agreeing
to take your name and raise a child with you?)

. . . . .

The wind is full disquiet, and the rain
raucous percussion on the windowpane,
and you are grateful. You are good and warm
and glad your girlfriend didn't go upstate
and leave you desolate for, God knows, weeks.
You love the heat of her; you love the storm.

THE HUMMINGBIRD FLASH FICTION PRIZE

THE 2023 HUMMINGBIRD FLASH FICTION PRIZE

The 2 0 2 3 Hummingbird Prize for Flash Fiction delivered exceptionally crafted stories — and resulted in some difficult decisions. Thankfully we had our fabulous judge, master of flash fiction Bob Thurber, to help us pluck the winning story from a nest brimming with talent. And, with a nest full of such high-flying Hummingbirds, the editorial team couldn't resist picking an Editors' Choice winner as well.

The winner of this year's prize is **Matt Lumbard**'s tender and lyrical 'Field's Nocturne No. 1 0 in E Major'. The Editors' Choice winner, 'Separate Worlds' by **Chip Houser**, engaged all our senses and kept us on the edge of our seats!

You'll find both of these delightful stories in this issue. Many congratulations to the winners and shortlisted authors:

'Sick Little Centaur' by **Alex Reece Abbott**
'Alternating Currents' by **Finnian Burnett**
'We Make Magic' by **Daniel P Douglas**
'Sheol Food' by **Marissa Fischer**
'Cupid's Rebellion' by **Cat Girczyc**
'Separate Worlds' by **Chip Houser**
'Field's Nocturne No. 1 0 in E Major' by **Matt Lumbard**

Thank you to Bob Thurber for making the toughest choices for us, and thank you to all the submitting authors for supporting *Pulp Literature*.

§

Matt Lumbard *is an American storyteller. This story is his debut publication.*

Chip Houser's *short fiction has appeared in* Bourbon Penn, PodCastle, Daily Science Fiction, *and various other markets. Red Bird Chapbooks published a collection of his micro- and flash fiction in 2 0 2 3 called* Dark Morsels. *He lives and writes in northern Colorado, where he also hikes, architects, and marvels at the miracles that are rescue animals. Find him online at chiphouser.com.*

Field's Nocturne No. 10 in E Major

by Matt Lumbard

Sonny wakes to the smell of coffee and the sight of his grandpa slipping suspenders over his shoulders, looking at the wood-stove, and muttering, "It'll burn itself out." He rolls over in his cot and looks through the little window to see fuchsia-blue breaking over the sky, realizing it is now day.

Gramp is tucking a pint of rye into his front overall pocket when Sonny says, "Seems a sight too warm this year, Gramp. Plus, Gram can't hear it now. Known you long enough to know you don't go for ghosts."

"You know me so good you'll know I don't break tradition," Gramp says, winking through a frown. His face shakes slightly as he bends to pull on his fur-lined boots, leather gloves, and the fighter pilot's cap that nearly covers his eyes, looking like a little kid in his oversized winter clothing and his let's-go-out-and-play countenance. "'Sides, I cored it last night. Ice is thick as a Tolstoy novel out there."

Before Sonny can pour himself a cup of coffee, Gramp flings the cabin door open and lets the snow yowl in, causing Sonny to dress quickly and forget his own gloves and hat. Sonny shimmies over to the piano and rolls it to the door, Gramp helping shoulder it down onto its side to where he's got the sled laid out and ready to land it. Still cloudily heavy-headed from last night's whisky and smoke-soaked playing cards, they step out of the cabin as white sunshine and bitter wind do more than a cup of coffee ever could.

Gramp swigs the rye heavy, tosses Sonny the rope like a hardened first mate, and without words they tie the big instrument and its stool to the sled like good clerks wrapping down a gift box. They cinch it tight, check its tautness, and Gramp lights a smoke. He takes the lead end of the rope over his shoulder and begins pulling with slow, sure steps toward the pond.

Sonny keeps his hands on the fading obsidian surface to steady it from tipping. He jokes and yells, "Mush!" over the wind, but Gramp doesn't turn back a smile, so he focuses on this picture of his grandpa with a hemp rope slung over his shoulder, bending tough against the wind in aged determination, cutting through the snow like a slow freight train, puffing a rolled cigarette into the wind like a steam whistle. The snow blades at Sonny's ears with shouted whispers. *Cold but not that cold*, he thinks, as he notices the snow packing rather than squeaking with their steps; then he looks up toward where the bare trees scratch the now yellow-white sky and where a V of geese honk through it, returning early for the season. And now again his mind turns to the pond, to the ice drill in the corner that did not look like it had moved, and to the amount of whisky and stories last night, hearing some for the first time. As they move forward he turns back and sees the curving lines of sled tracks from the warm small cabin and thinks of his grandma, but as the tears well up he shakes his head hurriedly and denies himself any further reverie, for he knows Gramp will not wait; he knows he must prevent this massive act of love from falling into the snow. Sonny looks up and already they are at the water, Gramp there expecting him to help steady it on.

They slide it out toward the centre as a falcon regards them from a maple at the pond's edge; this strange black mass and these two figures in the snow do not seem to belong where they tread. The piano slides easily now, yet they walk more carefully, shortening their steps as they try not to fall on the slick ice, until Gramp gives Sonny a look that means *this is a good spot*.

Tipping the piano onto its feet and placing the stool in front, Sonny steps back bleary-eyed, now knowing almost for sure what is happening, what he really knew was happening the moment he opened his eyes to Gramp's figure in front of the embers, and he lets himself feel everything. He thinks of Grandma, and of Gramp, and of their love as warm as wood-stoves in small cabins. A love that smelled of burning cedar and that now looks like a black piano on thin white ice. He tries to speak something to Gramp but he can't, because Gramp is perfect, sitting there on the stool, opening the key cover, turning to him and saying, "For her, for your grandmother," instead of the customary gaze into her eyes and, "For you, love. Happy birthday."

Closing his eyes, Gramp plays the first lightly wandering notes of her song as Sonny begins taking backward steps, fixing his view on Gramp while the music fills the ice air.

And then the cracks; just noises at first, no fissures; but Sonny turns away now to face the cabin and keeps walking with his eyes shut hard and his fists balled tight while the piano hammers roll with surety and beauty as he tries to convince himself that he didn't know what was happening when Gramp was up and dressed before him with the coffee on and the rye already half empty in his breast pocket.

Separate Worlds

by Chip Houser

The first time the earth tolls, we're all in our separate worlds doing what we do. We hear it, even through our noise-cancelling headphones, a single, skull-jarring clang like a big old church bell. Only it's everywhere, resonating through us, like our bones are tuning forks, tickling our insides. The ground vibrates, too. Not like an earthquake or anything. Just enough to make the leaves drawn in our latte foam quiver. It lasts maybe ten seconds, but it shakes our feeds all afternoon. Everyone posts what they were doing. Our top influencers share their epiphanies. Profound observations happen. Heartfelt resolutions are made. Some risk metaphor. It's all very unsettling and profound, until it's not. Eventually, after that initial mind-bomb, something else blows up, and we revert to whatever we were doing before the earth tolled. It was strange, yes, but ours are busy worlds.

Our parents' reaction to the toll? Watching their beloved 'news' anchors ask scientists all the smart questions. The scientists explain elastic deformation and electromagnetic fields and solar flares. The anchors nod sagely. Next up—after commercials—it's the politicians, promising investigations before pivoting to their usual talking points. Blaming the other side for the debt ceiling, guns, poverty, abortion. It's always the other side, always the same arguments. We get it, there's comfort in conviction, safety in entrenched positions. Except there are real stakes here, people. Like our future. Call us Gen X, but it's almost like they're wilfully distracting themselves from reality. Avoiding real issues like racism, inequity, the climate crisis. Yes, they're all real. Sleep on.

A week passes before the earth tolls again, like a reminder it's still here. Honestly, we have mostly forgotten. This toll is the same as the first, but its half-life in our feeds is an hour at best. The 'news' rehashes last week's segments, which ruins our vibe. We sink back into our comfortable, isolated little worlds.

The third toll comes a few days later. Our bodies feel a little strange this time, like it loosened our muscles or something. We probably need to move more. Everyone starts talking about exercise. Resolutions are made. Influencers post from their Pelotons in the latest brightly coloured fashions. Exercise is having a moment. Some of us even go outside. The streets are full of people toting signs like 'The End Is Near' and 'Lord Have Mercy'. Really? So annoying and misdirected. How about 'Go Electric' or 'Reduce Your Carbon Footprint' or 'Save the Planet'? Or, instead of shuffling around with your words of doom, how about starting a petition? Get some signatures. Be the change you want to see and all that. It's enough to drive us back inside, where our parents haven't moved from their couches. We go to our rooms, to our own screens, to our personalized realities.

The fourth toll is the day after the third. Our bones thrum with it. We're all sore, probably from all that exercise yesterday. Massages and hot tubs are trending. In our parents' world, so are churches. Their anchors interview priests, who read Bible passages about ringing church bells to banish demons. So medieval. The churches fill up, though, their small bells ringing and ringing and ringing.

The fifth toll comes at noon the next day, the sixth around sunset. Each one rattles our vertebræ, which feel loose. Bruised. Hot tubbing is still a thing. No one is talking about massages; they sound too painful.

The next day the tolling is hourly. We ache more with each toll. Our bones feel loose inside us. We seem to be the only ones affected by the tolling. All the animals — the *other* animals, that is — seem to be fine. Our buildings and bridges, cars and trains, all as sound as ever. Same with the forests and oceans and mountains. There are no tsunamis, no earthquakes, no landslides, no volcanic eruptions. Influencers and anchors and scientists and politicians and priests all share what they think is happening. No one agrees with anyone else's theory. If they're even listening.

The following day, the tolls happen every thirty minutes. From their couches, back for the evening from church, our parents confess all the wrongs they've committed. Especially the ones they worry messed us up. So awkward, all that navel-gazing. And misdirected. There's a global crisis going on, but not the one they think. We explain it's not Armageddon, it's us. Humans. We're the demons, and the church bells aren't working. Our talk doesn't go well. We end up in our rooms.

Now, the earth tolls every five minutes. We notice the shape of our skeletons as our bones soften. Walking becomes an awkward, sloppy agony. Even sitting is awful. Our pelvic bones bow and flex.

The tolling is constant now, wave after wave of pressure and sound overwhelming our senses. Our ears pop. Our heads ache. Our bones jitter inside us and come apart. We slump to the ground, our phones settling onto our gelatinous bodies. The constant vibration is comforting, though. Like we're the phones now, receiving notifications from the earth.

We don't hear the earth's final toll — our ears are just soft little bumps on our puddled bodies — but we feel it. One final, strong thrum that sets us quivering. The vibration fades into stillness. We can't post our feelings, but obviously this is a wake-up call. Even our parents must see that. Maybe even their 'news' people finally see it's time to do something. We wait for the earth to toll again, a different frequency or whatever science-type thing will rebuild our bones. So we can take action, so we can be the change the earth needs. We get it, we're ready. It's our turn to act. We wait, alone in our separate worlds. Expectant. Hopeful. But the earth stays still.

GET HOME SAFE

Sierra Louie

Sierra Louie is a writer and artist working on unceded Musqueam, Squamish, and Tsleil-Waututh land as she pursues an MFA in Creative Writing at the University of British Columbia. She writes across multiple genres including comics, poetry, and fiction. Her comics and artwork can be found on Instagram @sierralouieart.

GET HOME SAFE
by sierra lou

we should go...

SNAP!
come on, horse
RING
RING
what was that?

Zzzz

a sleeping giant...

is that you...
chérie?
tip toe

quickly
now
SNAP
squish
mreow...

if we wait
here long enough...

will he forget
about us?

some time later...
there was a beast after us. eventually, it fell asleep, but...
i lost all the fruit we gathered
i'm just glad you're here
it's so late...
yes, but you're home now

STELLA RYMAN AND THE LABYRINTHIAN PUZZLE

Mel Anastasiou

Mel Anastasiou writes the Fairmount Manor Mysteries, the Hertfordshire Pub Mysteries, and the Monument Studios Mysteries. Winner of a Literary Titan Gold award and longlisted for the Leacock Medal, Mel is also the author of two illustrated thirty-day workbooks on story structure: the steampunk-themed The Writer's Boon Companion *and* The Writer's Friend and Confidante. *For news on published and upcoming new works, visit her website, melanastasiou.wordpress.com.*

EMERGENCY

Stella Ryman and the Labyrinthian Puzzle

Stella Ryman, the octogenarian sleuth of down-at-heel Fairmount Manor, is on her own in her search for Thelma Hu, who is blind and vulnerable due to advanced age and hip surgery. Thelma's at a hospital somewhere in the city, the dodgy care worker Riley has been detained by the police for drunk driving, and Stella's bus trip downtown is nearing its end. At stake is Thelma Hu's future — it's well known that those who leave Fairmount seldom return. Stella will stop at nothing to find her great friend and bring her home.

When Thelma Hu was eighteen and all alone, she stood on her sea legs on the Coal Harbour docks, spitting distance from the boat that had brought her on a two-week journey out of China. She had a full purse in her pocket and was dressed in her best green silk dress with covered buttons at the neck. Even so, she knew she appeared an unlikely bride. The picture her grandmother had sent to her prospective husband had been, at best, optimistic. Furthermore, she'd seen a photo of her bridegroom. She knew he could do better.

Above her, seagulls shrilled like old aunties, and beneath her feet, between the dock's grey planks, sunlight flashed off water. The air smelled of fish, engine oil, sweat, and tar. A pair of stevedores pushed past her; the box they carried off the ship she'd sailed in on emitted a whiff of sandalwood, but it was gone before the aroma could break her heart for home.

Two hours' wait dockside supplied Thelma with all the evidence she needed to deduce that her fiancé must have arrived early, taken in a good view of her disembarking in her best dress, and decided that she would never look better than she did today. He must have said to himself, *no, I don't think so.*

Or perhaps … She laughed aloud, and a passing labourer scowled at her. Perhaps her fiancé had been so filled with the prospect of lifelong joy with a bride from his Chinese home that he felt dizzy with bliss and stepped under a bus, Thelma's name the last word on his lips.

Whichever it was, no one had come to meet her at the dock. Therefore, she had a choice. She could stay in this possibly accursed foreign city, herself an accursed foreigner, or else she must return home. She had the money for a return fare in her purse, slipped to her by her father before she walked up the gang-plank at departure. He, at least, would be glad to see her return.

Thelma Hu stood on the dock, her duffel resting against her knee. On her right, an oily slick washed between the great boats, their taut ropes singing against the bollards. On her left, wood and metal crates towered over stacks of sandbags, buckets and barrels. Between them lay the smoky, untried city. She put her hand in her pocket and took hold of her purse, because anybody with a head on her shoulders knew that city docks were excellent spots to be robbed. She turned her back on the ship and walked alone across the creaking docks, beneath the screaming gulls, above the greasy waters, away into the city.

It didn't take Thelma long to realize that life was all about money. People could be shipped away by family and abandoned by fiancés on docks, but money met you open-handed, stood by you, and sustained you. It fed you and sheltered you. It warmed you with a coat in winter and bought you flowers in the spring. Money didn't praise, but neither did it argue or bully. To get some, she took employment as a laundry girl and then found a job with a bad-tempered old mom and pop who disliked 'Chinese' but came to depend on Thelma to run every aspect of their corner store. Money she saved over twenty years bought them out when they grew too tired to carry on complaining; ten years later, money bought her a house. When, at nearly eighty, her eyesight began seriously to fail her, she wasn't bitter. If money could have bought her new eyes, it would have. The neighbours' girl, Cindy, walked with Thelma around the town for several years while her vision narrowed. Arm in arm, they strolled together down Quesnel Street so that she could, with effort, make out the cherry blossoms that bloomed in a long white arbour, lacy and streaming in the wind like a bridal veil.

At last she took herself to Fairmount Manor, because it was close to home. Once again she stood alone — or rather mostly sat, with few doings at the care home to spend her time on and no use for cash at all. Then Stella Ryman arrived with a new currency, one of intrigue and mysteries to be solved. Of confidences and jokes only best friends can tell. So it was that, until today, death — that second uncaring bridegroom — still had not come to meet her. Of course she knew death had the run of this hospital, but trapped as she was by post-surgical immobility and excellent nursing, all she could do was lie low and attempt to recover before death discovered her. She didn't fancy her chances.

Thelma lay in her hospital bed and dreamed she stood outside Emergency at a taxi stop, wearing her green silk dress with covered buttons at the neck.

Stella thanked the bus driver. She stepped onto the sidewalk by the taxi stop across the street from the hospital where she hoped to find Thelma Hu. It was a large, shambling, elegant edifice that reminded her of certain women she had known, those few who could pull on any baggy old clothes and appear ready to be photographed for *Vogue.* This hospital also reminded her of the day she'd given birth to Junie. It was a memory of not unmixed joy.

Soldier on, Stella. She and her early afternoon shadow crossed the busy road amid a train of nurses, identifiable by their white footwear, and downtown residents, distinguishable by their coolness. Odds and sods like herself were most likely visitors or, like Bethie earlier today, outpatients heading to hospital for treatment. Nobody was noticeably pregnant, and she remembered that for several decades now the dedicated women's hospital handled labour and deliveries. Women today were unlikely to do what Stella had done so long ago, *viz.,* turn up alone and in labour at this same hospital bus stop because she was saving her pennies and wouldn't fork out for a taxi. Stella, in labour, had waited under streetlights and outside the open gates. She'd braced against a brick wall mid-contraction, waiting for her husband to join her. In the end she'd gone in alone, but the beds had been full up that night, and reception sent her to general, a half-hour drive away across the bridge. She wondered, then and now, whether her husband had ever arrived here at all.

Back then, she'd longed to be inside this hospital to safely birth her baby Junie. Now, she was here to rescue Thelma and bring her home to Fairmount. Stella knew she was walking into peril to do so, for she was herself one swift professional diagnosis away from being drawn into the same protective mechanisms of eldercare that held Thelma here, far from her friends. For even though the police and helpful passers-by had not managed to stop her in her quest for Thelma, her own vulnerabilities remained in play. To illustrate,

1. Stella might tumble into a fugue state, and a medical professional could shoehorn her into dementia observation of some kind.
2. A terrifying diagnosis in unfamiliar surroundings might send Stella into a spin from which she didn't return. Stella might even forget her own name — and she had no identification, just a handbag full of travel accessories and a money belt stuffed with cash.
3. Thelma might, after surgery, meet with serious complications and be sent to palliative care. Would Stella have to feign dying to follow her?

Stella caught sight of her reflection in the hospital's front door. She could perceive no outward sign of agitation or uncertainty. She didn't look as put-together as the elderly woman next to her on the bus, but even in her pilling warm-up suit, her new cross-body handbag gave her an appearance of self-sufficiency and connected her visually to the world outside Fairmount Manor Care Home.

Stella took a steadying breath and walked towards the hospital entrance as if upon a razor's edge. A nurse in a smock bumped her on his way to the front door. He apologized.

"Not at all," Stella said.

"Are you all right? Can I help you find the front desk or anything?"

Since the invitation to inquire was wide open, Stella said, "Can I ask you a silly question?"

The nurse blinked. "Okay — if you promise it's extremely silly, ma'am."

"Could you tell me, please, upon first glance, what you think I worked at before I retired?"

"I used to play a drinking game like that."

"Sounds like fun. Now, if you don't mind, please tell me what you see." Stella stood tall with her thumb looped through the strap of her handbag.

He looked her up and down in her fleece warm-up suit.

"Ma'am, I'd say you probably ran a department at a nationwide sporting goods store. Senior staff."

"Gosh, you're good." Stella decided that if she was going to do a lot more lying — lying to good purpose, almost surgical lying, she reassured herself — she might as well start now. "Very close indeed. It was an independent sportswear outlet, though."

"Score one for me," he said. "I guess I haven't lost my touch."

Me neither, Stella said to herself.

She gestured to the hospital entrance. "After you, for I'm sure your patients await."

"Please, ma'am, after you."

He held the door for her, and she passed into a dingy reception room that possessed in the way of charm only its obviously distant construction date: the post-Edwardian wall sconces were half-concealed by nineteen-sixties suspended ceilings. There were a lot of labourers rolling trolleys filled with boxes and bits of unassembled metal shelving. Despite all the work going on, any progress here appeared rather bargain-basement in quality. However, Stella supposed that even a cheap upgrade would benefit patient care and staff efficiency. It was too bad this entry didn't get the sort of good, cheerful light enjoyed by the reception area Stella had observed earlier; however, they'd have to tear the place down to get that kind of open-concept look, and if they wanted sunshine as well, they'd have to demolish all the tower blocks surrounding the hospital to get it.

A woman in whites behind the laminate reception desk scowled at her computer screen. "It's about time," she said to the computer.

The computer beeped a warning back. The woman's frown deepened.

Stella recalled that when the young pregnant woman, whose husband had helped her park Icarus, had phoned from her cell earlier that day, the hospital computer had been down for some construction-related reason. What a bit of luck if it were indeed working properly now. She needed all the help she could get to find Thelma, because these hospital corridors, stairwells, and elevators were likely to be even more of a maze than the ones at Fairmount Manor, which was saying rather a lot. If the computer was indeed working, she might be able to pinpoint the location of Thelma's bed in this big rambling building, and even get directions.

Stella walked up to the desk. She tucked her thumb into her handbag strap. "I'm here to visit a patient with a hip problem."

"Name?"

Stella blinked at the receptionist. Normally she was happy to give her name, but normally she hadn't escaped from a care home, ditched her driver, and stolen said driver's car. But these were small-time crimes, so she did what any small-time criminal would do: she gave her mother's name instead of her own. "I'm Tanis Marie Seton."

"I mean, what's the patient's name?" The receptionist glanced up at Stella and then back at her computer screen.

Stella flushed. "Thelma Hu."

"Date of birth?"

Stella was ready this time, and gave Thelma's birth year, which was six years earlier than her own.

The receptionist whistled. "Not bad, not bad at all. Hope I live so long."

"Indeed," Stella said politely.

The receptionist shook her head at the computer and picked up a thick sheaf of papers that appeared to be a printout of names. Stella, with her librarian's love of order and her sleuth's impatience for progress, hoped to heaven the names were alphabetized.

They must have been, for after a pause the receptionist nodded. "Third floor. Bones, Muscles, and Joints. Ask again at BMJ reception."

"Thank you." Stella looked about for the elevators.

"But with all the work going on, I'd better phone up and make sure the corridor is safe for visitors." She picked up the phone, listened, and set it down again. "Nobody is answering. I'll phone again in a few minutes. In the meantime, you'd better wait."

"Oh, dear. Thelma needs me, you see." Stella looked around the chaotic reception area. "Can I wait in Bones, Muscles, and Joints reception?"

"Not possible, sorry."

"That's rather disappointing."

"We're in such a state, as you can see ..." The receptionist gestured at the workmen coming and going with trolleys and gurneys.

The receptionist would never guess from Stella's cooperative nod that she was secretly thinking up a plan to infiltrate Bones, Muscles, and Joints. Might not all this noise and movement of furniture, crates, and stacks of cardboard boxes provide cover for a stealthy raid past the receptionist and up to the third floor? Perhaps walking past the receptionist, hidden from her view on the far side of a big crate, in the manner of the Hope and Crosby *Road* films, would do the trick. Or maybe the receptionist would go to the washroom, and then Stella could make her break.

The receptionist—unwary soul—continued. "The café isn't even open, sorry."

"Thank you anyway, you're very kind. I'm just worried about poor Thelma."

"We can't allow visitors, as you can see."

"Nobody?"

"Almost nobody."

"What's almost?" Stella asked politely. "Just so I know for next time."

"Well, you could go up if you were her registered carer."

Stella started. "I am her carer."

"My goodness." The receptionist's eyes scanned Stella from head to cross-body handbag to toe. "I'm so sorry. Of course you can go up. I should have asked first."

Stella regrouped. "I should have told you."

"Not at all. I'll have to enter your name."

"I'm Tanis Marie Seton."

The receptionist wrote it down on her printout. "Right. I'll phone again to say you're on your way, so they'll be expecting you, Mrs Seton."

"Ms," Stella said.

"Ms Seton. Follow the blue arrows and take the third elevator in the second bank of elevators you come to. And do watch your step. There's so much debris around, and you don't want to end up in Bones, Muscles, and Joints along with Miss Hu."

"I'm certainly walking the razor's edge today," Stella said.

"Pardon me?"

Stella shook her head and thanked the receptionist. She followed the blue arrows past the first bank of elevators. However, when she rounded the second corner, the blue arrows vanished as if arrow guides had never been thought of. Instead there were a number of colourful lines, none of them blue, stencilled along the grubby tiles.

Stella followed the receptionist's directions as best she could remember them. She peered down the side corridors for banks of elevators, but saw none. The new painted guide lines led along the hospital flooring, side by side, but instead of indicating the elevators, they took her straight to a rank of three metal chairs set against the wall and bolted to the floor. The seating reminded her of the arrangement of the chairs in Corridor Park, where she and Thelma, along with the bitter crones of the Greek Chorus, passed their time at Fairmount.

In the first of the three seats sat a man about Stella's age. He wore the sort of cheery white moustache favoured by sports coaches, and a crisp blue and green tartan shirt beneath a three-season-weight tweed sport coat. A metal cane leaned against his knee. His hands rested flat on his thighs, and his slip-ons pointed straight along the coloured lines at Stella.

His face lit up. "There she is. Nice to see you."

Oh, dear. Stella said, "Nice to see you, too. You look like you're waiting for somebody."

He looked up and down the corridor. "I guess I'm waiting for you. Come and sit down, won't you? I'm expecting coffee, and maybe the nurse will bring two cups."

Stella revised her assessment. Here was not a demented person, but a gent of the loquacious sort she'd met so often in her youth and middle age. Generally, as they matured, they lost hair and physique but continued to score strongly in banter. She enjoyed his type, and moreover was grateful to them. In her young days, they had made up approximately eighty-five percent of the fellows who asked quiet girls to dance.

"Coffee sharpens my eyesight," he said, "so I can notice pretty women and offer them something to drink."

"And the possibility of a caffeine boost tempts us to comply." She looked along the corridor, feeling the full thrust of the day's exertions but wanting to get on. "Do you know the hospital well?"

He held out his hand. "My name is Wallace."

She shook it. "Stella. Pleased to meet you. Do you come here often? Of course, I hope you're well and just here visiting."

"No, you won't get rid of me as easily as that," Wallace bantered.

"Oh, you," Stella bantered back. These exchanges with this familiar type of fellow gave her the oddest feeling that a jazz combo somewhere nearby was about to kick in with 'Green Onions', and that somebody would bring her, not coffee, but a Singapore Sling. "I'm a bit lost, actually. I'm looking for a friend, and the directions the receptionist gave me ran out just about here."

"I'll have to write the receptionist a thank-you letter," Wallace said.

This guy was pretty good. Stella smiled but kept her hand on the steering wheel of investigative procedure. "I'm looking for a friend in Bones, Muscles, and Joints."

"It's a small world, Stella. I've just come from remedial therapy in Ambulant there. Was it your friend's hip as well?"

"Yes."

"And is this a woman friend?"

"Indeed."

"Well, well, so my luck is holding."

She laughed, as one did. "Do you have any idea how to get to Bones from here?"

"I do, as a matter of fact," Wallace assured her. "I have a clever way to get up there."

"That's wonderful," Stella said. Relief was a pick-me-up, better even than a coffee or a Singapore Sling or a Blue Hawaii, Stella's one-time alternate favourite. "Can you tell me?"

"Anything for you, Stella. Well, the corridors here are ridiculously convoluted, and when I was in for my hip operation — I got a pin, you know, and there were a few complications — "

"I'm sorry to hear it," Stella said.

"Well, I'm tip-top now, I assure you." He slapped his hip. "But for recovery, they send me out to walk, and even the fiercest outdoorsman would get stumped in this labyrinth. Even Daniel Boone."

"Or Davy Crockett," Stella added.

Wallace tipped his head back and sang 'Davy Crockett, King of the Wild Frontier', which had been ubiquitous in the mid-fifties. Stella joined in the second time round, but on the third iteration, she added, "Or Lewis and Clarke," because there was no song known to her with those explorers' names in it.

"Sure." Wallace was a little pink in the face from singing. "Anyhoo, I made it a little game. Want to play?"

Stella felt that she had already been playing quite a lot, but she said, "I sure do."

"Well, go round the corner"—he tipped his head to the right—"and find the next bunch of elevators. Come back when you spot them."

Stella rounded the corner, and the next, and saw three elevators. She returned to Wallace.

He said, "Get it?"

"Got it."

"Good. Now the next part is kind of tricky, but I think you're up to it."

"Think of me as Colonel Bowie," Stella said.

"Okay, Colonel, you're going to take the left-hand elevator and press the number three. Then, when you get out, you'll turn left again. You'll walk briskly for seven full seconds, then turn left, then right, then left, and you're there. Get it?"

"No."

Wallace burst out laughing. His delight was so obvious, and so entirely free from malice, that Stella laughed along with him. At last Wallace wiped his eyes and said, "I'm sorry, that's not the clever method, that's the ridiculously complicated method which I simplified with my clever method."

"Wallace, you are a card. Now, let's have the clever method."

"It's a kind of a mnemonic." He raised his eyebrows in a gesture that invited her to ask for a definition of the word.

But Stella was a big fan of mnemonics. "I like those. I use them to go to sleep."

Wallace nodded. "You're my kind of gal, all right. I knew it the moment I laid eyes on your lovely self."

"Thank you very much indeed. The mnemonic?"

"It's a marching song, actually. You might know it. *Left, left, left a wife and seventy children in perfect condition with plenty of groceries left, right, left.*"

Stella did know it. "I know it as *starving condition* and *gingerbread.*"

Wallace frowned. "Do you know, it works no matter what the children eat. You go to the elevators, take the one on the *left*, press three (that's the only trick), then you've *left* the second floor, and you get out at three, turn *left* out of the elevator, walk for as long as it takes to say *a wife and seventy children in perfect condi-tion*—or," he added fairly, "*starving condition …*"

"I do prefer *perfect condition.* But go on, I think I see the clever-ness of you."

He crowed like Peter Pan. "'*The cleverness of me!*' That's a good one, Stella. And the rest of the marching song …"

"… *with nothing but groceries …*"

"*left, right, left.*"

"Exactly. You turn left, right, left, and you're there. Say it with me?"

"I don't need to. I've got it." She had. "Thanks, Wallace. It's been a pleasure."

"Will you come back this way?" he asked. "Can I see you again?"

Stella hesitated. She wasn't sure she could easily reverse all those lefts. "I'll try. Thank you again."

He raised a hand, and she left him alone in the waiting area. She was sure he was sincere in wishing to see her again, upon her return from the third floor, but she hoped (mostly for his sake, and a little for her own) that somebody would give Wallace his coffee and take him wherever he was going. With a guilty pang, she realized she'd not even asked him where that was. But it was too late now, for here were the elevators, and there was the one on the left.

The doors of the left-hand elevator opened. Stella stepped inside, and the doors shut quietly for an old elevator in a decrepit hospital. She touched the button for three. The doors opened again, and shut, the elevator floor moved sideways, and presently she felt the slow rise of the ancient machinery.

Left, left, left a wife and seventeen children . . .

The doors opened onto a corridor and a big blue-painted number three. Stella stepped outside. She murmured, *"Left—*check! *Left—*check! And now, *left . . ."*

She turned left again. She made a rough calculation of Wallace's probable speed of movement and paced along with the next section of the mnemonic.

". . . a wife and seventeen children in perfect condition with nothing but gingerbread . . ."

Left. Right. Left.

She made the turns and found herself exactly where Wallace had said she would be.

There, the black and white melamine sign reading *Bones, Muscles, and Joints.* Here, the hand wash gel station. And next to it, the buzzer to press for entry into the department. But Stella saw at once that she wouldn't need to buzz, for the double doors stood open, propped back by cardboard boxes. Through them, the semi-gloom indicated that the hospital fluorescents were switched off. She detected the spicy odour of antiseptics and the sweet pine scent of cleaning fluid.

Stella stepped between the cardboard boxes and entered Bones, Muscles, and Joints. She walked along the central corridor past several empty rooms, each with four stripped beds. She passed nursing desks, where black-screened computer monitors stood. If there had been computer monitors on the *Marie Celeste,* she thought, they would have looked like these. She peered about her for Thelma Hu, or indeed any patient or staff member. The *Marie Celeste* began to seem less of a joke and more of an antecedent. Here indeed was a mystery.

A keen interest stirred within Stella, and with the practised eye of an experienced amateur sleuth, she surveyed the quiet aisle that ran between the patient rooms. She observed nothing out of the ordinary aside from the mysterious disappearance of every single person in the ward. There was nobody to ask where everybody was, nor any living soul from whom she might elicit the reason for the abandonment of these rooms and the missing patients, including Thelma Hu. Therefore, the investigation was wide open, and there were several ways in which she might approach it, some more difficult and demanding of hard thought than others. She decided to begin at the basic investigative level and move from there to the most sophisticated deductive strategies. After that, if she still hadn't made any progress, she would pass to the middling methods of the gumshoe investigator. She would leave gumshoe to last because, as its title suggested, it would require physical exertion, and she was quite tired. So tired, in fact, that she would very much like to curl up on one of these stripped-down mattresses, pillow her head on her hand, and sleep, like Ariadne on the island of Naxos. But she was not Ariadne. She was Theseus, and like Theseus she would soldier on with her search.

1.   Stella determined to begin with the most basic strategy of any search, employing methods that were obvious and not very sleuth-like but which would be foolish to bypass out of any Holmesian deductive arrogance. She called out, "Is anybody here? Doctor, nurse, or patient?" Her answer was the faintest of echoes, perhaps imagined. "… *patient?*" Nobody answered.

2.   She moved on to the most expert or extreme level of observation, a hyper-professional line of attack which required sub-numbering.

    2.1. First she must design a sturdy yet flexible theory.

    2.1.1 But what theory? Stella struggled to see any reason why all the patients and staff would disappear from what was, in an increasingly long-lived population, a high-use medical ward. Bodies outlived their joints these days, and nearly everybody she knew in the outside world had some Bones, Muscles, and Joints procedure done once they hit seventy.

    2.1.2 Moreover, Thelma had been listed as present in this ward. So it wasn't just a slow day in Bones, Muscles, and Joints.

    2.1.3 Therefore, the only logical reason to separate patients from their beds and nursing staff from their desks and monitors was because every patient had simultaneously gone for tests, physio, or procedures, and the staff had taken them there.

2.2 Therefore, Stella would lurk in the shadows until their return.

Stella paused to consider the positive and negative aspects of this articulated theory and its conclusion, *viz.*, that all patients and staff had gone to testing and would return in time. On the positive side, her logic was sturdy, for patients and nurses did go for testing and procedures. Moreover, it was flexible — because she had set no artificial timeline for their return. Nevertheless, the extraordinary coincidence the theory required — that everybody was somehow absent from the ward at the same time — was too much for a seasoned amateur sleuth like Stella. In fact, her study of Holmes, Poirot, Marple, Wolfe, and McGee showed that none of them believed in coincidences. Neither did Stella. Parallels, yes; coincidences, no. The implausibility of everybody vanishing at once glared at her like an investigative red herring. Therefore, she moved to

3. medium-level gumshoe investigation, which didn't start with a theory but instead required her to gumshoe around the place to make observations regarding the scene of the crime — or disappearance, at least. Above all, she had to keep an open mind. She must examine every tiny detail to see whether the puzzle came together. No elaborate numbering was required for gumshoe investigation, just a keen eye for detail and the discipline to draw no premature conclusions.

Observe. Note connections and anomalies. Draw no premature conclusions. Stella smiled. Gumshoe was her favourite investigative technique when she had the energy for it. She marshalled what vigour she could, polished her glasses on the hem of her fleece jacket, replaced them on her nose, and gumshoed into the first patient room on her left.

Even though the fluorescents were not operational and the window blinds hung closed, there was enough natural light from between the slats to see what clues might be discovered in this unoccupied room. The heavy blue curtains dividing the space from the corridor had been pushed back on their rails so that they bunched against the wall. The four beds, one per quadrant of the room, stood at odd angles, stripped to their impermeable pale blue covers. There were no stacks of laundered linens visible to the investigative eye. The floor had been mopped to a shine. The beds appeared to have been wiped down as well, and the bed to Stella's left, near the windows, bore a spray bottle of disinfectant. She peered at it. The white plastic bottle had only a small printed label and was evidently not a spray cleaner you could purchase from the supermarket or even hardware store. An in-house hospital brand, it seemed. This deduction was unlikely to add to Stella's understanding of the scene, but she made it anyway, without fear or favour.

More interesting, perhaps, were the twin objects lying on the bed to her right, where the corridor opened. These were a pair of white boxes, slightly grey around the edges, like plastic kettles after long use. They were free from dust. Their cords hung loose over the rail of the bed. A number of coloured buttons, including *off, on, reset, and call,* gave no hint of the electronic mission of these boxes. However, the lack of dust was inarguably a clue. Stella ran her finger along the bed rail and the blind slats. There was not much residue. Stella nodded.

Her first useful gumshoe clue: these hospital furnishings had been cleaned very recently, perhaps even today.

Stella walked across the corridor into a similar room, one which lacked windows. She hoped that Thelma had not been housed in here, for even though her friend was almost completely blind she perceived light and had a rim of vision outside her macular loss of sight. Thelma was happier near a window. This windowless room had four beds like the last, but had not been as well swept. Or rather, it had been swept, but the detritus was pushed into a corner. Stella shifted her handbag on its strap behind her back and bent down to examine the sweepings. These were made up of medical wrappings, crumpled tissues, a small plastic cup as for medicine, and a single turquoise sock, size large. Thelma was definitely not a size large.

In the next windowless patient room, Stella discovered more sweepings and a large mound of linens. Gingerly she picked through them to be sure they were used linens on their way to laundry, and she discovered a bottom sheet with a bloodstain showing clearly in its middle. This was the first bloodstain Stella had come upon in her role as an amateur sleuth, and she felt a professional satisfaction that the bloodstain, although not an indication of violence, was indeed a clue.

Indubitably. Observe all clues; draw no conclusions. Soldier on, gumshoe Stella.

Something made a pattering noise out of her sight in the corridor. This was the first sound she'd heard but for her own footsteps as she made her way around the Bones, Muscles, and Joints ward. It could only be somebody else's footsteps, speedier and quieter than her own. A nurse's soft rubber soles? Stella was about to call out when she identified the sound as one she had heard before, at Fairmount Manor. It was a sound she heard only when she was alone, as she was now. It was not soft shoes at all, but bare feet on institutional flooring.

Stella froze inside the fourth room of the empty ward. The sound of footsteps stopped. It would be just like Mad Cassandra Browning to tease her into a chase along an empty corridor. Mind you, she had no proof that the barefoot scurrier was Cassie. But if it was, her presence here would prove once and for all that she was a ghost. For there was one thing Stella knew about Mad Cassandra: she was nimble as a forty-year-old jazz dance instructor, and supremely unlikely to be admitted as a patient to Bones, Muscles, and Joints.

Stella moved past several more nearly identical patient rooms towards the centre of the ward. She left behind her the big blue curtains and discovered a number of doors. These opened onto two small offices, a staff break room, two washrooms, four storage rooms, and in the centre of the office area an enormous curving desk that backed up against the staff break room. This was truly a trove of investigative possibilities. Where to begin? She'd studied the empty ward bedrooms, so now she would investigate the persons in charge of the disappeared patients.

Stella set about examining the two offices. Inside the first she found a desk, a garbage bin, and a rickety shelving unit. A number of binders, mostly dark blue, lay in stacks across two of the shelves; the other three shelves were empty. This was, to somebody of Stella's lifelong experience in institutional settings, rather suspicious. She didn't think she'd ever seen an office where binders, booklets, and the paraphernalia of professions didn't crowd every shelf, leaving almost no room for the dying succulent that graced most work areas. Stella found this room's succulent in the plastic garbage bin next to the desk. Inside the bin she found papers and food wrappers, two pens — out of ink — and, beside the bin, a large brown cardboard box of the sort that housed items ordered for delivery over the phone, as Stella had always done, or via the internet, like the rest of the world.

There was no computer on the shiny-topped desk.

But this proved nothing, as laptops were portable. It would be no surprise to her to learn that staff took laptops with them when accompanying patients to treatments and tests, so as to complete work while they waited. But the details of hospital workers' schedules were unknown to Stella, and furthermore she was determined to keep an open mind.

She took her open mind into the second office. This room did not differ greatly in content from the first, although in arrangement it was less tidy. She found empty binders and loose papers strewn across the shelving therein. Moreover, the bin was on top of the desk, which was marked with sticky rings. In fact, the only dust was in the sticky substance. That was very interesting indeed, and Stella made a mental note. To Clue 1 — no dust in the patient rooms — she added Clue 2: the only dust was in the coffee rings on the desk of an obvious slob.

Stella didn't consider the office worker's untidiness a suspicious circumstance in itself. She knew only too well that institutional slobs were often among the hardest workers and most valued colleagues. And often they were the most tolerant and cheerful. Still, old dust not cleaned up in a dustless place might well turn out to be a significant piece of the puzzle.

She decided to check out the central desk area, where she thought one might normally find many fine professionals hard at work. Her first glance had assured her that the circular area was indeed unstaffed this afternoon, and her second now showed her that it was stocked with computer terminals: four of them. And all four showed blank screens. Stella reached out to turn one of the computers back on, but pulled back when she remembered that she was in a public hospital, and that patient records could be erased by an untutored hand as quickly as a teaching friend with literary aspirations had once erased 2 0 0 , 0 0 0 words of his unpublished first novel.

Stella leaned upon the desktop and cast a lynx-eyed look about the area. What to investigate now? Storage rooms? Washroom? Staff room?

As if in answer, she heard a voice whisper two words. The sibilant at the start sounded snakelike in the empty space. *Staff Room.* It might have been her internal gumshoe, speaking in her head; it might have been Mad Cassandra Browning, always a most helpful undead; or indeed, it might have been some other ghost in a building where a century of deaths might result in institutional haunts. But whichever it was, there was one way to test the suspicion that was expanding within her sleuth's brain (open-minded as it was).

Stella walked around the counter and pushed open the door marked *Break Room. Staff Only.* Here she found sofas, desks, plastic chairs, posters of a medical inspirational nature — *Nurses give TLC without prescriptions* — and more sweepings, but she felt no need to sift through these. Her attention was drawn to the sink and counter near the window. There were two closed cupboards over the sink, and another inspirational sign that read *I didn't go to nursing school to learn to wash your dishes.* She couldn't see a kettle, but somebody, not the slob in the second office, might have tidied it away. She opened the cupboards over the sink and found not a mere clue, but actual proof that her growing suspicions were correct. The gumshoe detective had all she needed now to solve the mystery of the missing staff and patients, for there was not a single box of tea, bottle of coffee, or packet of sugar substitute in the cupboards over the sink. All that remained to mark the passing of the nursing staff's consumables was an empty box of Wagon Wheels and a broken cup with an anatomically correct heart on it.

Her observations allowed only one conclusion: Bones, Muscles, and Joints was a closed ward. No matter what the receptionist downstairs had read on her computer, staff and patients, Thelma included, would not be returning here today, or possibly ever.

Stella left Bones, Muscles, and Joints and returned to the outer corridor. She looked to her right, which according to Wallace's mnemonic was the path back to the elevator, and to her left, where a glass door stood closed and unlit behind the usual pasted-up health-related notifications. Evidently this was a second abandoned department. It looked so much like the first, with its almost post-apocalyptic debris and darkness, that any further investigation was unlikely to yield anything in the way of new information. It was time to search out members of staff and interrogate them.

To get back to the elevator she turned right, left, and right, blessing Wallace all the time.

Stella had the elevator to herself again. She pushed what she thought was the button for the ground floor, but a moment later the door juddered open to reveal not the ground floor corridor with its painted arrows, but instead a brick archway leading into a patio garden.

Stella guessed the garden would have been designed to offer a haven of green to staff and visitors. She had pretended to be both, and was neither. But despite her age and situation, she was a sleuth and therefore curious. She left the elevator and walked under the arch to emerge onto the walled patio.

The garden was planted around its perimeter with rhododendrons and acid-green laurel, and rectangularly shadowed by the glass towers that grew everywhere downtown. Still, a ray of sunlight had found its way to pool on the bricks at the centre of the area. Stella felt herself drawn to stand in the sunlight, the way she was drawn at Fairmount to sit under the skylight in Corridor Park.

Stop here for a moment.

Take advantage of the unexpected.

Beauty doesn't last, you know.

Stella decided she could afford to give beauty a minute of her time before returning to her quest. She walked into the centre of the garden and rested there for one minute, and then another. Sunlight placed a warm hand on the top of her head and suggested she stay for a good long while. If she liked, she could move with the light as the sun made its way across the sky towards night.

Above her, the blue-grey city sky was reflected many times in the tower block windows around her. It had been a good idea to place a garden here, she thought, so that medical staff could escape from pressing duty and the needs of others. And, judging by the cigarette butts devolving under the laurel bushes, they did so. But not only staff could spend time in the garden, for patients capable of walking would make their way here too. Might they not come with visitors? She imagined children playing about the garden while their parents discussed issues for their own post-operative care. Yet there would certainly be patients who came here alone, to perch on the brick walls and study the sky while they weighed their choices and their chances. And maybe this sunlit space wasn't, after all, an encouraging place to consider one's mortality and chances for survival, because even she could feel in her bones the garden's siren call to stop, lie down, place her head on her hand, and sleep. Perhaps forever. The call to halt was sweet.

She wondered whether Thelma heard it too, wherever she was.

That thought jerked Stella out of sunlight's spell. She hurried back under the arch to the elevator. The doors opened. She stepped inside and found the right button for the main floor.

Soldier on, she urged the elevator. It shifted ancient hips and complied.

The doors opened on the ground floor and Stella stepped out of the elevator. She murmured, "*Left*—check!—*Left*—check! And now, *left* again." She wished she had such a clever mnemonic to help her find her way around Fairmount. It was not beyond possibility that Theo, with his background in teaching music at the university might help her to create one.

She approached the final *right* turning. She had been investigating the Bones, Muscles, and Joints ward so long that she fully expected to find the corridor seating area empty, but up ahead she saw Wallace, ensconced as before in the nearest of three chairs. Stella fantasized that Wallace had been set in place upon his seat long ago, like a friendly siren, past whom all who navigated these hospital corridors must travel.

Stella waved, and Wallace's smile lit his eyes and widened his moustache. He opened his mouth in song.

"Here she comes, Miss America."

Stella made the patting gesture that she had used in her career as an educator to quiet rooms of up to four hundred chatting students. It had worked with them but had no effect upon Wallace, who segued neatly into a rousing rendition of Guy Mitchell's 1953 hit 'Look at That Girl'.

She walked up to him, feeling self-conscious in a way that reminded her of her high school years, when a boy looked at a girl passing by his lockers the way Wallace was looking at her now. She sat beside him and put a hand on his arm.

Wallace finished up, *"… can't believe she's mine."*

"You're a very sweet person," she said.

"You found your friend, then?"

"No. The place was empty."

Wallace nodded thoughtfully. "Quite a few of us were wheeled or walked out of there this morning."

That was interesting. "Have you been sitting here so long? That's terrible."

"Andres brought me a sandwich. They're up to their ears today."

"Hospitals are up to their ears every day. But usually patients are in their departments, and Bones, Muscles, and Joints was like a desert island. What in this blue planet is going on?"

"Let's ask Andres. He knows everything."

Stella followed Wallace's gaze. An orderly approached, looking in his flapping white trouser legs like a friendly albatross. He smiled at Stella and helped Wallace to his feet. Wallace adjusted his cane and offered his free arm to Stella.

"All aboard," he said to her. Then he turned to the orderly. "Andres, meet Stella. She's just been to Bones, Muscles, and Joints, looking for a friend. But the friend wasn't there. Where might she be?"

Andres nodded in the direction of reception. "The ward transferred this morning. Don't you remember? You were last man out."

"Was I?"

"Yes, and you still haven't met with your therapist."

"My therapist Mahalia," Wallace explained to Stella. "She is tough but fair."

Andres nodded. "I'll get you in to see her once we're there."

"There?" Stella asked, a little louder than she had meant to sound. More quietly, she continued, "Andres, where are you taking Wallace?"

Andres looked at Stella with the kind but dubious expression that Stella was accustomed to receive from the Nameless Dear care workers who wouldn't dream of saying she was gaga out loud. "You know, of course, that this hospital is closing."

Stella stared at him. She did not know. But she thought it provident to say, "Of course."

Wallace said, "It was in the papers. But they didn't notify me of any change, so I thought I'd better show up here as usual. I guess the new hospital isn't as ready as they thought."

Andres nodded. "Computer glitches, all part of the moving blues. Plus, construction always takes longer than anybody dreams. So the new hospital isn't ready for patients yet, and you're all going to General."

"General?" Wallace said. "Goodness, now I see. You mean the general hospital across the bridge. Sorry, Stella. I thought he meant a general ward or something."

Stella felt the stone of inevitability form in her throat. What would she do now? She wished she had Icarus the Saab back, to wing her out of here and on to the next hospital. She thought of returning to the taxi stand, and what it would take out of her to direct a taxi driver. Then there would be hours of searching at General, which, at three times the size of this hospital, was bound to be overburdened and thus underorganized.

"Easy mistake to make," Andres said cheerfully. "General this, general that. Let's go, Wallace. Your transport awaits. Nice to meet you, Stella. Watch out for the movers with their trolleys, won't you? They ought to have indicators and alarms."

Wallace said, "Oh, Stella's coming with us."

Andres began, "Only caregivers and family members ..."

Wallace said cheerfully, "Oh, Stella's a family member."

Stella wished he had said *caregiver*, as she was registered here as such and was comfortable with the designation. But she supposed that *sister* was not too far a reach.

Wallace said, "Stella is my fiancée."

Andres blinked. "Congratulations."

"That counts as family, right? At our age?"

"At any age."

"That's the attitude that I like to see. Right, Stella?"

"Er, yes," Stella said.

"That's my girl."

She tucked her arm into Wallace's, and they followed Andres along the corridor.

At first Stella couldn't make out what tune Wallace was humming. But when she did, she thought, *of course*. Of course it would be the wedding march.

They made their way towards what transportation this hospital would afford them as it sank like Atlantis into the sea of age and obsolescence. The end of institution, of history, of good care and long service.

Amid the bustle of workmen pushing equipment-laden trolleys, the receptionist directed Andres, Wallace, and Stella to the exit in Emergency, on the far side of the hospital building. When they stepped through the double swinging doors, they found in the busy parking lot a twelve-passenger van shining in the afternoon sun. The side door of the people carrier showed a half-dozen patients drooping in their seats, with room for several more. The driver's sweaty brow was creased, as if his day had been long and the traffic bad. He hooked an elbow over the back of his seat and motioned to Andres to hurry up.

Wallace said, "I'm not going in that."

Andres said, "There's plenty of room."

"But I wanted to go in an ambulance."

"This is an ambulance."

"It's not a proper ambulance, with me lying on a stretcher and Stella here holding my hand." He winked at Stella.

"Just get in and buckle up, Wallace," Andres said. "This is the best transport we can offer."

"Either way, I'm going," the driver said. "You folks are more than welcome to take the next ride."

Stella saw her safe route to Thelma at General going up in the smoke of Wallace's burning desire for romance. "I'll hold your hand," she said. "Give it here."

She took Wallace's hand in hers. It was damp — romantics' hands were always damp in her experience — but not unpleasantly so. She led him to the van, and Andres helped them both inside.

"Everybody buckled?" The driver asked. "Better check them, Andres. I feel like I've been driving cats and chickens around all day."

Andres checked, while Stella gave the driver a stony glance. She said, "If you have to compare patients to animals, I would prefer to be a horse."

There was a laugh from behind her, and an elderly woman spoke up. "I would like to be compared to a wise owl."

Wallace said, "Me, a polar bear."

The driver said, "All right, all right, and I'm a pig. I apologize. Traffic's been a bastard. I mean, it's been tough."

"How long have you been doing this?"

"Since seven this morning," the driver said.

"That is a hard day for a driver," the woman behind Stella said. "Maybe we could all sing to keep the driver's spirits up."

Wallace asked, "Does everybody know 'Look at That Girl' by Guy Mitchell?"

Stella had, in her career in the public school system, ridden with many a field-trip driver, and she knew something of their feelings towards passengers belting out songs on the journey. She said, "I think quiet would be kinder. Let's all look out the windows and enjoy the ride."

The driver said, "I think I love you, lady."

Wallace said, "Hey, buddy, she's mine."

Stella sat with her handbag on her lap and her hand in Wallace's, gazing out the window and appreciating the quiet rumble of the van. Outside, the greater world rolled by, and inside at the back, one of the passengers fell asleep so that his stertorous breathing connected the van's riders with the engine noises and the outside traffic.

All told, it was a soothing atmosphere, and several more passengers dozed off, including Wallace. His grip on her hand loosened slightly. Stella spent the last five minutes of the ride liberating her hand in small increments of movement so as not to wake him. She succeeded in freeing herself just as the van pulled into the large semi-circular drive behind a similar vehicle, also jammed with patients. Stella folded her hands across her handbag and watched the back bumper of the van in front of them rise with the exodus of its passengers. Once empty, it drove off, and Stella's driver rolled forward to the hospital's reception doors. The driver stepped down to help his passengers out the side door. He held out a hand to Stella. She gazed at Wallace, asleep in the seat beside her.

She said, "Thank you, Wallace." But she said it very quietly. Wallace didn't wake, but lay with his head back and his mouth open, peaceful as a sleeping bridegroom.

Stella let the driver help her down from the van and thanked him. Before anybody else could alight and follow her, she hurried into the noisy, congested reception hall and lost herself in the anonymity of the crowd.

This afternoon, the city general hospital's foyer boiled with patients in chairs and visitors on phones. Stella was not a patient, and only nominally a visitor; she stood uncertainly in the centre of the hubbub and wondered how best to proceed.

Soldier on, Stella. Her fatigue had eased over the course of the van journey, and she felt charged with a watchful edginess that she supposed all sleuths, amateur and professional, must experience when nearing the final stage of their pursuit. She judged it vital, now, to tighten rather than loosen the reins of investigation; not so much as a matter of investigative style. Of course style, like logic, carried its own justification, but more than that, she felt she must guard against overconfidence, for, having stolen Riley's Saab and employed various falsehoods and aliases, she had perhaps profited from rather good luck. She fully intended to play out her role as Miss Marple, but she was conscious that she was nearly as much Papillon, absconded from institution without possibility of parole, and a whisper away from recapture.

She stood tall, straightened her fleece jacket, and ran her thumb along the bulging line of the travel wallet tucked under her trouser waistband and inside her underwear. She rested her thumb on the crossbody strap of her new handbag and felt as ready as she'd ever be for what she fervently hoped was her final approach to Thelma Hu.

Caution murmured that she should minimize contact with persons in authority. She decided this time to eschew the lineup for the receptionists and try one of several free-standing computerized map kiosks to find the Bones, Muscles, and Joints department at this latest hospital. There were short queues for every computer map console except the one nearest her. Stella soon saw why: a small boy was planted in front of the screen, feet apart and shoulders hunched. His air of immobility and reluctance to share was instantly recognizable to Stella from her four decades in the elementary school system. She looked around the crowd for his parents—another thing teachers learned was that modern parents, like adult bears in wilderness settings, never wandered very far from their offspring in public places. And the ones you could not see were the most dangerous.

She approached the little boy, observing his clever swipes and prods at the kiosk screen. He appeared to be about eight years old, and he was nicely togged out in a golf shirt and coordinating shorts.

She cleared her throat.

He did not look up.

She said, "How interesting that there are video games here for visiting children to play. I call that very thoughtful."

The boy shrugged and swiped at the screen.

"My grandson Derek tells me updates are very important. Do they update these games to the latest releases?"

He shot her a disbelieving glance. "It's not a game."

"My goodness, but you seem very good at it. An expert, as far as I can tell."

"It's just a map."

"A map?"

"Yes. It's pretty stupid, but there's nothing else." He scowled at the screen.

"What's the best thing about playing with it?"

"Nothing." He held a thumb on one of the coloured sections of the map, and after a moment it began to blink.

"Is it broken?" she asked.

"I didn't break it. Blinking is all it does."

"May I please have a turn?"

He looked her up and down and grimaced. "What do you want?"

"Well, just to try it."

"I mean what do you *want?*"

"Oh, I see. Well, I'm looking for a friend named Thelma Hu. Can you find her for me on the screen?"

"Nope." He turned back to his swiping. "It's a map. They don't put people on a map."

"What about finding the ward for bones, muscles, and joints?"

He prodded at the screen. "No such place."

This seemed to Stella impossible, given Andres's testimony about the movement of patients from the Bones, Muscles, and Joints ward in the downtown hospital to this one. She was about to ask the boy to look again when two adults approached the console. She cursed untimely parental proximity and moved two steps backwards. In an effort to fit in with the crowd, she glanced up at the clock above the doors and then fished in her handbag as if looking for her car keys or her phone. However, it was obvious from the way both golf-shirted parents were staring at her that her stratagem had failed. She decided that if they spoke fiercely to her regarding her interaction with their son, she would reply in French, which she had taught at the elementary level and in which she'd grown in proficiency over the course of several summer holidays spent near Carcassonne.

But French was not required. Both parents pinned her with scowls and dragged their son away from the map kiosk. Stella heard the mother ask, "What's the rule?" Stella knew the rule, and she was certain the boy did, too. But he didn't recite the rule. Instead he looked back at Stella over his shoulder and called out, "I found it. It's called Complex Joints at this hospital, not Bones and Muscles."

The family group moved off towards the outside door. The boy had left the computerized map blinking and unreadable, but he'd gifted her with a solid clue. She looked around for signage for Complex Joints, wondering why on earth the powers that be would call the department Complex Joints when it was named

Bones, Muscles, and Joints at the last hospital. One would think the same knees and hips in the same people in the same city would have the same name. And one would expect that there would be enormous, easy-to-read signboards to offer directions in case computer map screens were blinking and unreadable. She would even have welcomed arrows to point the way.

A woman about her own age walked up to her. She wore a green cap lettered with white that read *Community Aid*. "Can I help you find what you're looking for?"

Stella was about to ask her where the Complex Joints unit might be found, but she recalled her vow of caution. Hers was a simple enough inquiry, but she reminded herself to keep her cover intact while she made it. *Don't get cocky,* she told herself. A voice deep inside her answered, *But what if I like being cocky? It's got me this far, hasn't it?*

She straightened her back and hooked her thumb onto her handbag strap. "I'm a carer for a patient recently transferred to Complex Joints from the downtown hospital."

"I see. Would you like me to help you find your client?"

"Do you have time? All these people …" She looked about her for a queue of people waiting for help from the woman in the green hat, but nobody was looking at either of them.

"I have time."

Their eyes met, and Stella understood. You could put an official green cap upon an elderly woman, but you couldn't make a busy world ask her for help.

"Please do show me where Complex Joints may be found," Stella said. "Thank you."

The woman's cheeks flooded with colour, and eyes lit up. "Follow me, dear," she said. "I'm Cynthia, by the way."

"Call me Tanis Marie Seton," Stella said. She twitched her warm-up jacket straight and followed Cynthia down several corridors and up two separate elevators towards Complex Joints. Along the way they left behind them the human scents of sweat, cologne, and deodorant for the odours of hospital suppers heavy on the broccoli. The shift in smells created for Stella a compelling connection between these corridors and those of Fairmount Manor, and it significantly raised her hope that she would soon return to Fairmount with Thelma Hu safely in tow.

Cynthia was a whiz at inquiry, easily the equal of one of Sherlock Holmes's Baker Street Irregulars. One intense minute questioning staff at the nurse's station in Complex Joints brought Cynthia results. She led Stella straight to Thelma's room, waved away thanks, and left Stella there.

Thelma's room was apparently meant to hold four beds, but in a pinch it could, and today did, take six. She scanned the recumbent patients for Thelma and spotted her in the bed nearest the window. Stella made her way among the beds and scattered visitors standing about bedsides. There was no place for visitors to sit, for the usual chairs were stacked and relegated to the corridor to make room for the extra beds. But the fates had left Stella a boon: a visitor's chair overlooked and turned sideways between the window and bedside in Thelma's corner. Stella wiggled herself into it and gazed down at Thelma's sleeping face.

Afternoon sunlight through the window lit the white threads among the black in Thelma's hair. Stella's friend lay on her back, and her small figure raised the coverlet only slightly. Thelma's skinny, knobby fingers lay folded across her breast in the attitude Stella always associated with a composed and self-determined death—as so often, she referenced Tennyson's 'Lady of Shalott'. Her heart pounded and then gentled when she made out the slight but certain rise and fall of Thelma's breast beneath the cotton blanket.

Stella let out a long breath. With it went the fear, unspoken even to herself, that she was too late: that Thelma had taken a lonely and permanent departure from hospital, that she had released her grip on life the way she'd let slip away the ship that could have returned her to China and her family. Thelma was still here. Alive. She hadn't left without Stella.

With care not to wake her friend, Stella manoeuvred her legs up to rest on the bed. She leaned her head against the window and set her elbows on her armrest, hands clasped around the strap of her travel handbag, which like her had reached the end of the journey. Stella fell into a light doze, and when she awoke, the light in the room read late afternoon. Thelma was staring up at her from her pillow.

"Is that you, Stella Ryman, or is that your ghost?"

"I was dead tired, but that is exactly how far I intend to go in that direction." Despite a heavy neckache and one foot asleep on the bed beside Thelma, Stella felt a surge of energy. "Wait a minute. Let me get my foot working."

She wiggled her foot around and put both feet on the floor in the tiny space beside Thelma's bed. There she got a charley horse and stretched that out, groaned, and sat down. Thelma chuckled, and the man in the bed across from Thelma's looked up from his phone and applauded. He said, "I got that on video. Do you mind if I post it?"

Stella knew she had looked ridiculous, and said so.

Thelma said, "You didn't look ridiculous."

How would Thelma know? But there was no polite way to ask that question of a woman with macular degeneration and only a fingernail's worth of peripheral vision. Stella shrugged. "I guess it doesn't matter what I look like."

The man with the phone said, "Come and look. She's right, you don't look ridiculous."

Thelma said, "That's because you have to be ridiculous to look ridiculous."

Stella frowned. "Everybody's ridiculous sometimes."

"Everybody *feels* ridiculous. That's quite a different matter."

The man nodded. "Just watch the film. Even if I put in clown music, you just look resilient and even rather dignified. But funny. I think I've got a winner here, if you say okay to post."

Stella was about to say *no, thanks for asking though,* when Thelma said, "At our age, we should never miss a chance to be discovered by Hollywood."

"Oh, go ahead," Stella said.

"I just filmed your agreement." The man grinned and zoned back in on his device.

Stella turned to Thelma. "Are you all right?"

"Huh. What exactly do you mean by *all right?*"

"Have you seen a doctor? When's the operation? Can I come in with you?"

"You're a little late, Stella Ryman. They put a pin in my hip around lunchtime."

"Good heavens. You mean you're all done?"

"Yep," Thelma said, and Stella didn't miss the note of victory in her tone, as if she hadn't avoided all help for her hip for weeks. "I'm all done. They've already had me exercising it in bed. They call me . . ."

A nurse crossed the room and stopped at the foot of the bed. "We call her Xena, Warrior Princess. Fastest walker over ninety we've ever had."

Stella said, "She's only eighty-eight."

Thelma said, "I want to go home right now."

The nurse crossed her arms. "You're going nowhere tonight, young lady. There's such a thing as postoperative blood clots."

Thelma said, "There's such a thing as hunger strikes, too."

Stella pulled the nurse aside, out of range of Thelma's hearing and the phone man's as well. "I'm Thelma's carer, Tanis Marie Seton."

A snort from Thelma's bed told Stella she hadn't moved far enough after all. "At her age, I'd like to get her home as soon as possible."

"I understand your worry, Miss Seton …"

"Ms," Stella corrected her.

"… Ms Seton, but we will certainly not release her tonight."

"Exactly how likely are blood clots?"

"Not likely. But we watch for them all the same."

"But the very elderly are at risk for hospital infections."

"We'll send her home as soon as possible. But she'll have to pass a couple of simple tests."

"What kind of tests?"

"We have a little set of stairs, and most importantly she'll need to get to the washroom on her own steam."

"Let's go," Thelma said.

"Physio will conduct the tests," the nurse said. "And Physio has gone home for the day."

The nurse hurried out. Thelma thumped her head on the pillow and growled at the ceiling. Stella touched her arm, and

Thelma shook her off.

The phone man said, "This will cheer you gals up: I've gotten likes already. I'm going to edit you to music."

Nobody had edited Stella to music in her whole life, not even parents who videotaped their children's school winter concerts. She said, "Can I see it?"

He said "Betcher bottom. I'm Jase."

I'm Stell," Stella said, and then remembered she was using her mother's name as an alias. "I mean, I'm Tanis Marie Seton."

"I like *Stell*," Jase said. "Okay to use it?"

At the speed this fellow worked the internet, she guessed that she was *Stell* out there already. It was her own fault for having misspoken her own alias, so she said, "That's fine."

Thelma shook her head. "I'm so glad you're here, *Tanis Marie Seton*, even if we both leave this hospital feet first from the fun of it all."

Jase looked up from his phone. "Feet first? Stell, what's going on?"

"Nothing that isn't always going on," Stella said. "Thelma is just making light of death."

"You look in the pink, but now you've got me feeling guilty. I should have asked: is there any reason this film will come back to bite you in the ass?"

Stella imagined the Warden viewing Jase's video of her in the hospital. But saying so would only make Jase feel sorry, and to what good? "You know, at my age and Thelma's, the film would have to move pretty quickly to reach us in time to bite us on the ass."

Jase tilted his head, and Stella saw the penny drop. "Can I film you saying that?"

Stella looked from Thelma, who was listening to their banter with lively interest, to Jase and his phone. "Does that phone actually phone?" she asked him.

"Can I film you asking that?"

"Just listen for a second. I need you to call somebody. Or somewhere. But I don't have the number."

"Sure. Who?"

"*Who* second, *where* first."

"Ready." Jase held up his phone.

Before Stella could instruct him further, Thelma threw her bedclothes aside and sat up on the edge of the bed.

Stella said, "I'm sure it must be too soon for you to move around, Thelma."

"That's not what the nurse said. I'm supposed to do everything I can to move around on this pin in my hip. Better to get my joints moving too soon than too late. Film this, Face."

"Jase," he corrected her. He held up his phone. "I might be onto something here. I'm not sure anybody else is doing this kind of video."

Thelma slipped down to the floor and felt her way barefoot along the side of the bed. Stella looked around her for Thelma's red silk slippers but couldn't see them. The woman in the next bed huffled in her sleep and rolled over, and Jase filmed away with a steady hand. He said, "There's never been a better time to be a filmmaker."

"Where's the toilet?" Thelma demanded. "I want to do the toilet test."

Stella stood, ready to search out the facilities, but the nurse returned first.

The nurse said, "Blood clots."

Thelma said, "Toilet."

"You're not going home tonight, but the toilet is straight ahead. Go on and walk." The nurse helped Thelma into the corridor and set her up with a walker. "I'm right behind you."

"Not too close," Thelma said. "And while I'm in there, you go find those little stairs I have to climb."

"You're not going home tonight, Mrs Hu."

"It's Miss."

Thelma and the nurse clattered out of sight.

Stella returned to Jase's bedside. "How are you feeling?"

"Not as good as Thelma," he said. "She got a simple pin and I got a whole new hip. I'll have to climb the stairs too, I guess. Do you still want to make that phone call?"

Stella told him who to call. It took Jase about ten seconds to tap in his requests, and then he handed the phone to Stella.

"Fairmount Manor, front office."

Stella didn't recognize the female voice on the other end, which was just as well. Even so, she disguised her voice with a smoker's rasp. "This is Tanis Marie Seton phoning from the General. I'm in Thelma Hu's ward, and I need to speak to Riley right away."

"How is Miss Hu?" The voice asked.

"Thank you, she's recovering well. May I please speak to Riley?"

"He's working ..."

"We're all working, dear," Stella said. "I really must speak to him in regard to some paperwork for another patient, Stella Ryman."

"My goodness, is Mrs Ryman all right?"

"*Yes.* May I please ...?"

"I'll get him."

A long moment passed while Stella gazed out the window at the lowering light of evening and wondered just how much more she could accomplish in a single day. She was as tired as an old shoe, but to her surprise she didn't feel drained of all energy, but rather ready for anything if only she could take a short nap first.

Riley's voice sounded over the line. "Who *is* this?"

Stella said, "I'm so happy the police let you go, Riley."

"Not so loud, Mrs Ryman." Riley lowered his voice. "And do you mind very much telling me exactly where you put my car?"

"All in good time." Stella told him precisely what to do. His initial fury would only make his eventual quiescence more satisfying and help in some small way to create a better balance of fairness in this youth-heavy world.

Sometime in the middle of the night, in that overpacked hospital room, Stella discovered that even with her feet up on Thelma's bed, she was so far from feeling comfortable that she could hardly remember what the word meant. In an attempt to placate her outraged back and neck, she reminded herself of incidences of worse physical torment.

1. There was labour, of course — eight stunning hours of it when Junie was born.
2. She was unlikely to forget the mid-seventies flight to London in which she had been seated between two strangers with pointy shoulders. The plane had stopped twice on the fourteen-hour journey.
3. And she well remembered one night in her extreme youth when she had slept *al fresco* on a sloped clearing with nothing but a homemade sleeping bag between her and a lot of roots and stones.

These memories were not, after all, much help. She stared across Thelma's room at the fluorescent-lit corridor. The glowing green walls united with her discomfort to make her feel like she had been tied up and was waiting for mobsters to put her to sleep with the fishes.

She returned her gaze to Thelma. This was a woman so tiny that she made the single white bed look big enough for two. Without further mental discussion, Stella crawled onto the bed, curled up next to Thelma, and slept until the nurse shook them awake.

Stella wiggled off the bed. When Thelma didn't open her eyes, the nurse patted the older woman's thin shoulder. Stella peered up at the nurse's face, trying to read there what she hoped to see — and not what she feared had come to pass.

The nurse shook Thelma's arm a little harder.

Thelma made a gentle sound, and then another, a little like a cough.

The nurse looked at Stella. "What did she say?"

"She didn't say anything." The sun through the window felt warm on her shoulders, almost as good as a friend's embrace. "She's laughing."

Thelma struggled up from the pillow onto her elbows. "You nurses are complete pessimists."

The nurse put her hands on her hips. "I love the funny patients. Especially the ones who pretend to be dead. They get my blood moving of a morning." But she helped Thelma to sit up, set her into her walker, and led her along the narrow crowded way among the beds to the corridor.

"I'll be back," Thelma said. "Just let me show those stairs what's what."

"You're the boss," the nurse said.

"I don't want to be the boss," Thelma retorted. "I want to go home."

Stella had appreciated Thelma's pretence at dying, because she felt rather like death herself. She longed for her Room 34 at Fairmount Manor, and for the dining room with its cups of weak tea, cold toast, and the dubious company of the Greek Chorus. She was grateful that the staff had let her sleep undisturbed next to Thelma all through the night, but she felt it would be stretching her welcome to ask for breakfast.

She fumbled on the floor for her travel handbag and slung it on. She said good morning to Jase and the other patients and stepped outside the ward, walking slowly at first until her joints loosened. An old fellow in a green *Community Aid* hat directed her to a coffee stand near the reception area. She brought one for herself and one for Jase, who invited her to sit on the side of his bed. Here she awaited Thelma's return, watching the videos created by Jase on his little phone screen. The coffee went down easily, which was fortunate, because when Riley stormed into the ward and called Stella by name, the cup she dropped was empty.

By ten that morning, Thelma, like the grumpy trooper she was, had climbed every step with a cane, mastered her walker, and independently visited all the washrooms in the ward. Jase had filmed much of it, although when she went to the washroom, the nurse made him erase every second of the footage. All the while, Riley leaned against the wall with one foot crossed over the other and drank cup after cup of coffee.

At last, with Thelma's walker folded in the trunk of Riley's Saab, all three of the Fairmount Manor party rode silently towards home. Up front, Riley rested one forearm across the steering wheel, riding the clutch and clomping down on the brake. In the back seat, Thelma dozed. Stella was secretly delighted to be reunited with Icarus the Saab. She passed the journey wide awake and deeply engaged in plotting their smooth return to the care home. Despite going what the director might term 'absent without leave', there was little danger she'd be tossed out of Fairmount, which, like a country, was obliged to take back from abroad even its most wayward citizens. However, Stella had no wish to reveal to Mrs Perdita Warren her actions of the day before. She was certain they'd be added to the slate of delinquencies the Warden of Fairmount Manor kept on her. It was not only Stella's pride that was at risk, but also her scope for activism: every time Stella made a well-founded complaint and petition on her own behalf and that of the other residents, that slate was the Warden's best weapon against Stella's demands. Stella took stock of the cases that would soon need defending: the return of justice and peace of mind for the beleaguered Rose Corridor women, as well as Dotty's mystery cat, who must inevitably be discovered. And that would be a can and a half of worms.

Riley turned right with a jerk of the wheel, and Stella decided to break the silence.

"I see you successfully retrieved your car, Riley."

He shot her a look that said *mistress of the bloody obvious.* "You noticed that, did you?"

"I was worried about your licence after the police incident."

She saw his fists tighten on the wheel, and he gave the brakes an unnecessary snub. "Yeah, I have to appear in court. Thanks for that."

"Don't blame me. I suggested you drive off for a sandwich, not a series of beers. What did Mrs Warren have to say about it?"

For a rejoinder, Riley swerved right onto a side street, where the Saab came to a halt behind a garbage truck. Riley swore, reversed into a driveway, and retraced the Saab's path. It was answer enough.

She knew he wouldn't tell the Warden. Stella covered her laugh with a cough. She didn't like Riley, but she had much to thank him for. Primarily she was grateful for his help in returning Thelma to her side and driving them safely homewards — well, fairly safely, considering Riley's reckless ways at the wheel.

But she had by no means forgotten that he was responsible for certain wrongs at the care home. She wondered what she ought to do about it. She had no doubt that Riley's arrest for drinking while in charge of driving one of Fairmount's residents was a career-buster. And, for an underdog rebel for residents' rights, this kind of power, over a care worker only loosely fitted with a conscience, was as good as money in the bank. Out of respect to her own hard-driven but operational conscience, she promised herself not to overdraw on his cooperation.

She covered another smile by gazing out the window at a corner mall. "I know this area well. I used to buy wine at that shop." Too late, she realized she'd put her foot in it.

"Rub it in, why don't you?" Riley asked. "Please, if you have any more alcohol jokes, do trot them out."

"Riley, I promise I wasn't referencing your arrest for drunk driving. I only meant we must be about five minutes away from Fairmount."

"Maybe," Riley answered. "Or maybe eight. Or nine."

Stella allowed him his grump without comment. Like Churchill, she believed that no victory should be entirely one-sided.

Laurel hedges and cherry trees flicked past the Saab's window. These had formed part of the area's well-established flora throughout Stella's life. The cherries, past blooming in this season, fluttered new leaves against the late spring sky. She wondered whether she'd live to see them return to full flower, parading down the side streets like pretty prom-goers; but she'd asked herself exactly the same question the year before, and the year before that. *No bathos required here, Stella Ryman.*

Stella had nearly forgotten the feeling of return home from travel. She recalled coming back from afar on school holidays, and how buzzy her brain always felt fresh off a flight — a very different sort from her flight from Fairmount the previous day. In those earlier times, when she still owned her house, the taxi would take her home via these same streets, shaded by these same cherry trees and lined with the same laurels. When the taxi neared her address, she would pass paper money to the driver and would haul her own suitcases through her front gate. The yard always overgrew its bounds while she was away, and the blowsy, uncontrolled boughs and blossoms would lean out to touch her as she passed, their manners most personably welcoming. Now her house was gone, sold with everything else when she came to Fairmount Manor; but strangely, just now she felt that she was coming home. How amazing, that she could feel such a deep-seated, joyful expectation at the thought of setting her feet on Fairmount's familiar soil, or rather its grubby flooring.

But she mustn't forget that her return today was different in ways that the feeling of coming home couldn't disguise.

1. She didn't own Fairmount as she'd owned her own beloved house. She didn't even own Room 34 in Daffodil Corridor.
2. She had no solid plans to take future voyages. (Although, she did have her new travel handbag, with those travel gadgets still in their dollar store boxes.)
3. Most importantly, this was the first time she had returned home with a friend she'd not left with.

She squeezed Thelma's arm and leaned forward to speak to Riley at the wheel. "Thank you for driving us. What a treat to take another ride in your good old Saab."

Riley's icy silence melted at the compliment to his car. "The Saab's definitely a cooler ride than any ambulance. More like a hero's return, right?"

He patted the dashboard. Stella remembered doing the same to Icarus the Saab the day before. She also remembered feeling stylish at the wheel. The next time she stole a car, she would have to remember to wear sunglasses.

She peered ahead through the windshield and made out Fairmount Manor's boxy shape among the trees and shrubs ahead of them. As the car drew nearer, she saw that a grey-haired fellow was standing out front. For a breathless moment, Stella felt certain the man was Theo, somehow made aware of their return and poised to welcome them home. But proximity revealed a younger man than Theo. He was, in fact, a member of the care home's board, one of those who had visited at breakfast-time the day before. She couldn't remember his name, but surely he was one of the two real estate agents on the board. When Stella had first laid eyes on this fellow, he'd been measuring Fairmount's road frontage with a long tape on a roller. Now, he stood with his hands on his hips, and she followed his gaze up to Fairmount's black tarred roof. It was mossy on the ridges and ragged, as Stella well knew because the leaky skylight cut into it over her chair in Corridor Park. This member of Fairmount's board of directors was doing no harm standing and staring like that, but she couldn't imagine he was up to any good either.

Riley drove past the man, pulled on the brake, climbed out of the Saab, and stretched. He strolled around to the trunk, where he'd put Thelma's folded-up walker.

Stella shook Thelma awake.

"We're back. So those who leave Fairmount do sometimes return."

"Stella Ryman, let me be. These car seats are more comfortable than any piece of furniture in Fairmount Manor, including my bed."

"You can't live in a Saab, Thelma. We're home, just like you wanted."

"It's always something, isn't it?" Thelma stirred herself to sit up. "Well, I guess I'd better say thanks for coming to get me when I was alone."

"I was the one who was alone," Stella said.

Thelma scowled. "I forgot to ask you. Did you get me anything?"

"Oh. Well, I got you home."

"Ha. But I'd be ashamed to visit somebody in hospital and not bring them at least a box of almond cookies."

Behind them, Riley banged the Saab's trunk closed, and the walker clattered onto the driveway.

Stella brought her handbag around to her lap and opened it. "I did bring you something. Here." She handed Thelma the second money belt.

Thelma held up the belt to one side of her face, where Stella knew she had a scrap of vision. She ran thin fingers over the belt's zipper. "What am I going to do with a money belt? You never found my money, did you?"

"Not yet," Stella admitted. "But I do have some money for you. I can't show it to you right now."

"Don't let that Riley see. He'll take it quick as you can bite. Did you get me anything else?"

Stella glanced out the car window at Riley, who was crouched over the walker's wheels. Over on the grass by the roadside, the real estate fellow with his offensively possessive posture was making his way towards the far corner of Fairmount. "I did get you another gift. But Riley might see it if I take it out of my bag right now."

"Don't show me, then. Just tell."

Stella knew Thelma would hear the smile in her voice at the thought of the third, most precious of the travel gadgets in the Krownkind Security Triple Pack she'd purchased at the Dollars4More store. "I brought home travel door locks. One for each of us. We can lock ourselves in anywhere, whenever we want."

"Lock ourselves in the bathroom?"

"Could be."

"But we don't want the locks to be confiscated. We'll have to be careful."

"Discretion is certainly the better part of privacy."

Thelma frowned out the window at Riley. "Can we lock other people up?"

"I think not, sadly."

"Well, we can lock them out, anyway. If we're tricky about it."

"My friend, I believe that's our specialty."

Riley opened the Saab door. "You've arrived at your destination, ladies. Thelma—I mean Miss Hu—your walker awaits you."

Riley fiddled with the walker's bar, and Stella seized the opportunity for a quiet word with him.

"I trust, Riley, that you'll make sure the Director doesn't find out about my travels yesterday. Nor about your . . . little trouble with the police?"

Riley frowned. "Perdita Warren can't see farther than her nose. I'd do a better job running this place. In fact, *you'd* do a better job running this place. Why are you in a care home, anyway?"

"I'm old. That's why."

"You're not that old. Why are you here?"

Stella came as close as nothing to responding with the truth, *viz., the excellent life I'd designed for myself turned on me, towered up, and chased me four blocks over into Fairmount care home.*

Instead she said, "Let's get Thelma to her walker, shall we?"

Thelma, aided by her cane, stood upright and glared at nothing.

Riley said, "If you're tired, Miss Hu, sit in the walker seat. It makes a little wheelchair, see?"

"Don't say *see* to a blind woman."

"You told me you're not blind. You have macular degeneration."

"I think I know whether I'm blind or not."

"Sorry. Here, let me help you into your walker."

"Did you test it?"

"I set it up."

"You set it up, so you sit in it first."

Riley huffed a breath, shook his head, and sat down. The walker buckled underneath him, and he caught himself on the Saab's back fender before he hit the ground. Stella imagined how Jase would have enjoyed filming the scene; to hide her smile she left Riley to his axle-and-lever articulations and walked towards Fairmount Manor's front door.

Through the glass she saw that the foyer was occupied. Two people stood within, and as she neared the doorway she recognized Dr Terry and Reliza, engaged in furious, nose-to-nose discussion. What a crying shame that nothing had changed for these two part-time lovers.

She reached the door and was about to rap on the glass when she saw Reliza raise a hand and touch Dr Terry's cheek. They turned to see her, and Stella's relief and pleasure at Reliza's gesture of peace must have shown on her face, because their faces lit up, too.

Dr Terry held the door open and waved Stella inside. "Are you all right, Mrs Ryman?"

"I'm fine," Stella said. "Thanks for asking."

Dr Terry nodded. "Good to see you looking fit. Does Riley have your hospital paperwork?"

Stella said vaguely, "It sounds likely. Reliza, how are you?"

"The better for seeing you back at Fairmount. And how is Thelma?"

"A very good nurse said she'll need physiotherapy."

"I know an excellent physio," Reliza and Dr Terry said in unison.

Stella smiled. Things in this quarter of the world of romance were looking up. She wondered what had tipped the scale. It might have been their shared worry over Thelma and Stella herself, but more likely their reunion could be traced back through the simple rhythms of romance: the ups and downs, draws and resistances, riffs and fugues that make young love such an enduring pursuit.

Stella said, "I must ask you two for something, and Riley can't know I told you."

The doctor and care worker exchanged a look. Dr Terry said, "I might tell that guy the time of day, but that's it."

Reliza nodded. "What do you need?"

Stella looked over her shoulder. Riley was engaged in wheedling Thelma into her walker seat. He couldn't possibly overhear. "It's about Rose Corridor. Don't let Riley dispense their meds anymore. He's been withholding meds when he doesn't like cleaning up accidents. So it might not be enough just to give him the cold shoulder. I'm afraid he'll bear watching."

Dr Terry frowned out the window at Riley, who was helping Thelma into the walker's seat. "I'll see if I can have him fired."

Stella wanted to say *better the devil you know and can keep an eye on*, especially when Riley would doubtless go to another care home where they didn't know his little ways. But she could see it for the poor argument it was, so she only said, "You'll have a hard time proving grounds for his dismissal to the Warden on my say-so, but good luck to you. What about the diaper situation in Rose? Any more threats from the board to send the incontinent ones to other homes?"

Reliza shook her head. "Rose Corridor as a group is wearing pull-ons so that none of them is singled out to leave Fairmount for long-term facilities."

Heroes. They were everywhere, weren't they? Stella tipped a salute in what she hoped was the direction of Rose Corridor.

She supposed there might come a day when that particular band of sisters would break up, but today was not that day.

Theo appeared at the entry to the foyer. He tugged his yellow cardigan straight around his middle, and a smile crossed his dear face. In fact, he looked happier than Stella had seen him for months. An urge to show him her new travel handbag and relate to him yesterday's adventures overwhelmed her, and she stepped up beside him and slipped her arm through his. They exchanged smiles of easy friendship, for she and he were unified still by the shared architecture of this institution, by similar, quiet senses of humour, and by the bone-deep patience of career educators—hers in the elementary school system, his at the university. Together they watched Thelma make her way up the little shrub-lined path to the front door. She did so on her own terms, pushing the walker before her rather than riding in it, while her cane teetered on the walker's seat. Riley hurried around her to open the foyer door.

Above the rattle and roll of Thelma's walker wheels, Stella heard the click of the front door as it shut the lot of them inside Fairmount's foyer. It was the sound of closure, and with it her pleasure at returning home vanished. Now she felt that she had lost something vital and irreplaceable: her citizenship of the outside world. Yesterday she had belonged out there — a senior citizen, but a citizen. With the click of the door, that entitlement was gone as if she had never left Fairmount at all. As if her final connection to a normal life was severed. Tears pricked her eyes. *Soldier on, Stella.*

Outside the window, Icarus the Saab's door opened on its own. Maybe that simply meant that Riley should take more care than to leave doors imperfectly closed. But a second later she recognized the message of the Saab, which was that she'd got her situation all wrong. She had not left the outside world, for she was still connected to it through this very Saab and their shared adventures. From there, the Saab was connected to the road, which was connected to the city, wherein lived people she knew, however long- or short-term these friendships had been, because they were social networks unbound by proximity or even chronology. Along with a lifetime of connections she'd made in school and out of it, she now knew the young couple expecting the baby, the Voltaire-reading shop clerk, the bus-riding woman with her perfectly tied scarf, Wallace and Andres (she felt badly about abandoning Wallace, but that guilt was a connection too), Jase and his phone, the nurses and the Community Aid volunteers in their green hats. All these persons were connected to each other as of yesterday, and, if you investigated that network, the source of these connections was none other than Stella, right here in Fairmount Manor. She stood up straight, gripped Theo's arm tighter, and hooked her other thumb through the strap of her travel handbag. Nothing and nobody could take away her pleasure in her adventures over the past day. Nor could anything diminish her success in finding Thelma and returning with her, rather as if Stella's friend were a sort of elderly Golden Fleece.

The staccato patter of good-quality high-heeled shoes approaching at speed heralded the arrival in their midst of Mrs Perdita Warren, Director of Fairmount Manor. Her arms were full of flowers, as they'd been the day before when she was adorning the bulletin boards in anticipation of the Board's visit. But these blossoms were not cut out of paper. These were the real deal: a grand bouquet of orange and red gerberas, drooping lilacs, and spiky pink carnations, all tied up with straw ribbons.

"How pretty," Stella said.

The Warden clacked to a stop. She looked from Thelma to Theo to Stella. "These are for you."

She pushed the overwhelming mass of flowers at Stella, who let go of Theo's elbow to take hold of them.

"Who sent me flowers?"

The Warden dug in her suit jacket pocket, pulled out a small envelope of the sort that florists attach to deliveries, and held it out to Stella. Stella passed the flowers to Theo in order to examine the note. She observed that the envelope had been opened, no doubt by the Warden herself. She imagined the curiosity and condescension with which the Warden would have read Stella's personal correspondence, and burned with displeasure. She pulled out the card; had Vaughn sent her a bouquet to follow the gift of money he'd given her the previous morning? In her day, when boys sent flowers and a gift within a twenty-four-hour period, the girls called it *rushing*. She opened the card and found that somebody had handwritten the words *Thanks, Stell!* and what was certainly not a V for Vaughn but a J for Jase.

The Warden said, "Another grandson, perhaps?"

"Just a friend. Thank you."

One might have thought that Mrs Warren's manners, if not her ruddy job description, might have prompted her to welcome Stella and Thelma back from hospital. At the very least she ought to congratulate Thelma on her rapid recovery from surgery. Instead, she turned on her expensive heels and walked swiftly away. Stella exchanged a look with Riley, who winked at her, jingled his car keys, and walked out the door towards his Saab. Reliza took the flowers from Theo; Jase had certainly gone overboard with the bouquet, which hid the young care worker's upper body from view. Reliza offered to find Stella a vase of an appropriate size.

"I'll put them on the bureau in your room."

Stella thanked her. "Let's have them in the dining room instead. And keep my name out of it, if you don't mind."

Reliza smiled and walked in that direction. A few blossoms fell from her arms as she walked. Dr Terry followed and retrieved the fallen flowers, like a hair-gelled Ruth gleaning the field where a pretty Boaz passed.

Stella's heart lifted. She took Theo's hand, gave it a squeeze, and let it go; but he took her hand back in his. His gesture reminded Stella that despite inequities, aches, and pains, these later years of life weren't always tragic, nor were they the second childhood the world promised for your old age. That particular promise always sounded to Stella more like a threat, as if in her old age the world would give her something to cry about. She smiled to herself, and then spread the smile around to Thelma, who couldn't see it, and Theo, who returned it.

Stella helped Thelma turn her walker into position to take on Fairmount's circuitous corridors. She and Theo stood on either side.

"Are you sure you're up to this?" Stella asked. "I don't want you to fall down and end up with a second pin in your hip."

"Stella Ryman, you heard that good nurse tell me to walk. I told her about *you*" — she jerked her head towards Theo — "walking everywhere around and around Fairmount. She said you'd probably live forever."

Theo thanked her, and Thelma grunted. Stella appreciated the value of being one of three friends. Two friends together had fun, the way a bicycle with its two wheels was a delight to ride. But three was a solid number of chums, like a tripod or one of those three-legged stools common to homes from prehistoric to Swedish Modern times. Three standing together could endure any strain.

They strolled — Stella and Theo — and rolled — Thelma — their winding way towards Corridor Park. When they rounded the corner, they found that all the bright paper flowers the Warden had lately stapled to the bulletin boards had been unstapled and strewn about the floor. Above this scissored garden, the Greek Chorus sat in a prim row against the wall of Corridor Park. Iolanthe and Lucille looked up from their crewel work at the three new arrivals, and Sally lowered her golden snips.

Iolanthe said, "My goodness, how lucky. We were hoping that you weren't dead."

Lucille said, "Of course, nobody's irreplaceable. I learned that at work."

"But nobody's interchangeable either," Iolanthe added. Sally, the Nodder, nodded.

Stella took a second look at the paper flowers lying on the floor, and deduced the reason for them.

"All this for us?" Stella gestured at the display and clarified for Thelma, who would see only scraps of colour at the periphery of her dying vision. "They've spread flowers in our path, Thelma."

"I don't believe it," Thelma said.

"Unless it was you, Theo?"

Theo shook his head.

"Thank you," Stella said to the Greek Chorus. They exchanged looks.

"Well, it's more or less a sop," Lucille said.

"An indication of our appreciation," Iolanthe said, although she was in general one of the least appreciative persons on earth. "And we rather hope that you'll take on a case for us."

"A case?" Stella felt her ears prick up.

"Have you seen that real estate fellow with his measuring tape? There's nasty business happening here."

"I smell money." Lucille, with her long career as a loans officer for a major bank behind her, narrowed her eyes.

"Everything always leads to money," Thelma agreed.

"And where there's money, don't think you won't find a rat." Iolanthe pointed her needle at Stella. "We've been watching, and we have several motives and suspects."

"We're not the sleuths, though," Lucille said. "We are the sniffers of smoke."

"There's smoke, all right," Thelma said. "I still want to know where all those mahogany tables got to when they exchanged them for the aluminium cheapies we've got now. Those tables were worth a little bundle in the furnishings trade."

"It's all connected, that's what we think," Iolanthe said.

Stella nodded. "And there are missing funds budgeted for food. I saw some of the numbers when I stole the Warden's papers not too long ago."

"Do you still have them?" Iolanthe demanded.

"I do." She had hidden them in her bureau under her least favourite floral knit shirt.

"Well, why haven't you brought these people to justice already?"

Lucille said, "Stella's too busy gadding about the city. Look at her with her new cross-body handbag."

Thelma clacked her walker wheels against the floor. "If it's a really big fraud, it's going to be outside as well as in."

Funny business with prime real estate property — property dedicated for the use of one of society's most vulnerable populations — would indeed be a serious matter.

Theo helped Thelma into her chair with her cane and pushed the walker against the wall. Stella sat down on her own chair at Thelma's side. She felt happier to be back under her skylight — what she sometimes thought of as the last stop on the bus route of life — than she could have imagined possible before her voyages outside. The adventures of the preceding two days had proven that even here at Fairmount Manor, nothing was over until you actually died. And what a comfortable thought that was. It was an understanding unique to her in her situation here at Fairmount, to be enjoyed with Thelma at her side and Theo nearby, raising his hand in adieu before leaving to walk Fairmount's twisting corridors. Even though they had little control over their surroundings and were bound about by the strictures and structures of institution, they and all Fairmount residents comprised a society unto themselves. The world outside, getting and spending, wasn't interested in their dull days in here, in the lives they'd led in service to their communities and greater mankind. But the Fairmount residents knew what lives they'd led. Some had lived adventures beyond the imaginings of following generations, and some had lived microcosms of small sweet love stories and family drama. Theirs were stories like old books with thick pages that most people these days would never read. If she looked at it from that angle, it was clear that Stella, Theo, Thelma, and the rest of Fairmount's residents could boast the great treasures of privacy and social independence, accorded by society to only the most boring of folk. And the beauty was that, with untold rich lives behind them, they didn't have to be boring if they didn't want to. However, they could be as restfully and obnoxiously dull as they liked, and no care worker or visitor would blink an eye or weigh in with a remonstration. As long as a resident could toilet herself and present a bland facial expression to the Warden, she could operate beneath the radar of administration. In a way, Stella was freer now than she'd ever been in the course of her busy life. She was also closer to death than she'd ever been, but lately she'd been questioning the linearity of a lifespan. Arguably, she'd been nearer to dying

1. when she was twelve, and the safety strap on a fair ride snapped;
2. at thirty-eight, the time the car ahead of her had been T-boned; and
3. not to mention the repeated and nearly infinite fatal possibilities that had never terrified her, for the hammer of death had fallen and missed her, just out of sight.

Stella smiled. Theories of mortality were welcome to wheel about her mind indefinitely, even though conclusions often eluded her. She longed to ask Sartre whether, existentially speaking, and given the dangers of modern traffic, all human beings were not equidistant to their demises. She also desired to interview Descartes, not in regard to 'I think therefore I am'—she had ceased to credit this credo since arriving at Fairmount—but to talk over his more generous opinion that life was geometrically a ray rather than a finite line segment. She wondered whether Descartes might not agree that everybody's lifetime was made up of an infinite number of points. Mathematically speaking, because the number of points on the line was infinite, nobody's life should ever quite reach its end. Furthermore, although

Descartes had not weighed in on this extrapolation so far as she knew, Stella believed there were as many unsolved mysteries in the world as points on a ray.

She said, "The next game's afoot, Thelma. Let's take a minute to rest our bones, and then we'll have at this new mystery."

"I'm with you, Stella Ryman. But let's take as many minutes as we have bones," Thelma suggested.

Stella tilted her head back, gazed up at the blue sky above her skylight, and counted her bones and her blessings.

§

Here ends Stella Ryman and the Search for Thelma Hu. *Coming next from Mel Anastasiou, the first act of a new paranormal tale set in 1991. Because Metallica had a great song that year about a spirit that takes hold and won't let go, the new novel is titled* Take My Hand: A Ghost Story.

THE HAUNTED GHOST

JJ Lee

JJ Lee has been our most prolific feature author over the years. His monster-chaser Bekker appeared in Pulp Literature issues 8, 24, and 34. In addition to the pen and ink drawings that accompany his stories, JJ has provided us with two cover paintings: Fallen Angel, based on Robert J Sawyer's story, in Issue 7; and the iconic killer teddy bears of Pulp Literature Issue 2, which featured his story 'Built to Love'. Author of the multi-award-finalist memoir The Measure of a Man: The Story of a Father, a Son, and a Suit, *JJ* writes and records a Christmas ghost story for broadcast every year for CBC Radio. We published one, 'Desdemone', in Issue 17, Winter 2018, and are delighted to close out our tenth-anniversary issue with another.

$\mathcal{T}$HE HAUNTED GHOST

A CHRISTMAS STORY

Five o'clock on Christmas Eve, Cath and Clare shoo out the last-minute shoppers. It always annoys the customers of Burrard Books.

"But most stores stay open until six."

"I know, I know," apologizes Clare. "We used to. But not anymore." Clare doesn't explain why. She guides them to the door and locks it.

Napkins and paper cups are scattered everywhere. Since 1957, the year it opened, Burrard Books has always served shortbread and cider on Christmas Eve. It's a good tradition, and Clare happily tidies the shelves and display tables.

Cath sums up the sales. "Less than last year."

Three months from now, at the end of the fiscal, they'll close the shop forever. Cath sighs. She puts on a red scarf and looks out the storefront window. It's snowing.

Clare rummages through the drawer under the register. She finds CC's old reading glasses and sets them on the counter.

Cath is impatient. "Do you really have to do that?"

Clare's face turns solemn. "Yes." Like the shortbread and

cider. It's tradition. Next to CC's glasses, Clare places a book bound in red Moroccan leather with gold foil decoration. "It's so beautiful." She says this every year because it is.

Cath turns out the lights, but Clare leaves a small brass desk lamp lit on the counter. Before the pair go out the door, they call into the darkened bookstore. "Merry Christmas, CC."

Burrard Books, with its volumes of recipes, Penguin Classics, murder mysteries, biographies, and memoirs, becomes quiet. That's when CC emerges from the back room. She likes the shop best when it's empty. She shuffles to the counter and stands before her reading glasses and the book bound in red Moroccan leather.

Cath and Clare have always been so thoughtful, even as young girls. She used to play with them in the storage room. They would make forts out of empty shipping boxes. It was fun, but the games always tired CC out. Maybe that's why she never had any children herself. But if she had, she would have much preferred daughters like Cath and Clare.

CC begins to flip through the book, and she waits. At five fifteen, the store grows cold.

On the avenue, a car makes a U-turn. Its headlights streak the shop with beams and shadows.

The boy appears.

CC smiles. "Mr. Five-Fifteen."

The boy ignores CC and begins to browse through the mystery and crime shelves. He likes the pulpy stuff. Mickey Spillane, Ellery Queen, Ed McBain, and anything with Alfred Hitchcock on the cover. The boy drops them on the floor, one at a time.

CC speaks out loud, but she's almost talking to herself. "I could always set my watch to you. Every Saturday, near closing time, you would come. Five fifteen. Every Saturday." Her voice dies in the boy's silence.

The boy holds up a title. He frowns at the price. He only ever carried fifty cents.

"It was always so hard for you," CC says. "Having to choose only one book."

The boy nods and lets it fall.

"Will you not finally take *this*?"

She holds up the book bound in red Moroccan leather. She still remembers that day.

December 24, 1966. Another Christmas Eve, a Saturday. Back then, the store remained open until six. The boy came in, as he always did, at five fifteen.

CC thought he had lifted a book into his jacket. "What are you doing, you rotten little boy?"

He ran away. The book from his coat lay on the floor. CC picked it up.

She saw the title-page calligraphy, the hand-drawn illustrations and maps. There were thirteen stories typed on folded half pages that were stitched together and bound in covers made out of a Rice Krispies box.

The boy had fabricated his own book.

CC says, "When I realized my mistake, I sent it to the bindery." She holds up the book bound in red Moroccan leather. "These are your stories. I waited for weeks and weeks, hoping you'd come back, but you never did."

The boy shakes his head.

CC wipes a tear from her eye. "Were you the boy in the paper who was struck by a car?"

The boy nods.

"I thought so. Then the next Christmas Eve, books kept falling off the shelves. And I kept putting them back."

The store is quiet. The street is still. Frost creeps across the storefront window.

CC says, "It has always been you."

The boy nods.

CC says, "Won't you take the book? After all these years?"

He shakes his head.

"I read it every Christmas Eve. Detective Tombes is a very resourceful hero. He's a very insightful protagonist."

The boy smiles.

"Come see the book."

The boy sidles up to the old bookseller. He touches the red Moroccan leather. She turns the pages for him. His smile grows wider.

She asks again, "Won't you take it and forgive me?"

The boy shakes his head.

CC is pained. "Cath and Clare mean to shut the store down forever. You won't be able to visit anymore."

The boy steps back and offers his hand to CC. He says in the softest of whispers, "I forgave you many years ago. Now forgive yourself. Take my book, and let us remain here no more."

On Boxing Day, Cath and Clare open the shop.

Cath picks up the paperbacks scattered on the floor. She complains. "Every freaking year."

Clare tends to the counter. She places CC's old reading glasses back in the drawer. Clare will really miss CC when the store is gone.

She scratches her head. Where's that darn book?

THE ARTISTS

Melissa Mary Duncan
Cover artist, Cheers

Melissa Mary Duncan is a Canadian-born fantasy painter whose work explores the rich expanse of northern European faerie and folklore. She works primarily in pencil and watercolour but recently dusted off her acrylic painting skills for a gallery exhibition. The show, 'Witches, Bitches and Canny Women', with fellow artist and sculptor Lynne Fahnestalk, will take place in the autumn of 2023 at the Mission Art Gallery in Mission, BC. With a wink, Melissa will tell you the title of the show is a nod to her grandmother, a jailed British suffragette. Melissa blames her fascination with folktales on a misspent youth in her local library. There she lost hours poring over the seemingly endless stacks of cloth-and-gilded volumes of fairylore published during the golden age of book illustration. She blames her obsession with creativity on her family: her mother the drama queen, her father the rocket scientist, and her elder brothers who became actors and media personalities. Her sister became a singer. Melissa was a bit of a late bloomer when it came to wanting to be an artist. As a broke single mother, she took it into her head one day to paint her daughters' bedroom walls with flowers and fairies. She has never looked back.

Melissa's work reflects her love of history, the natural world, and humanity. Her favourite time of day is twilight. Her favourite season is fall. Now that she is in her seventies, her favourite drink is decaf tea — Murchies, of course. Melissa enjoys historic reenactment, British cozies, folk music, and filling a blank page with her Once Upon A Time imaginings. She lives in historic New Westminster with her writer husband dvsduncan and their cat Major William Catastrophe.

Sierra Louie
Illustrator, 'Get Home Safe'
Sierra Louie is a cartoonist and MFA candidate at the University of British Columbia. Her comics can be found online @sierralouieart on Instagram, and, if you find yourself in Vancouver, at Lucky's Books and Comics. 'Get Home Safe' is inspired by stories like 'Thumbelina' by Hans Christian Andersen and *The Secret World of Arrietty* (2010), directed by Hiromasa Yonebayashi. Sierra is happy to announce that, with the completion of this comic, she has finally learned how to draw a cat.

Mel Anastasiou
In-house illustrator
Mel Anastasiou loves drawing for *Pulp Literature* because she loves the stories she illustrates. She draws in black and white, working from imagination and inspired by details from Renaissance compositions. You can find illustrations, writing tips, and news about her books and novellas at melanastasiou.wordpress.com, and see more of her artwork on Facebook at Bird and Branch Artwork.

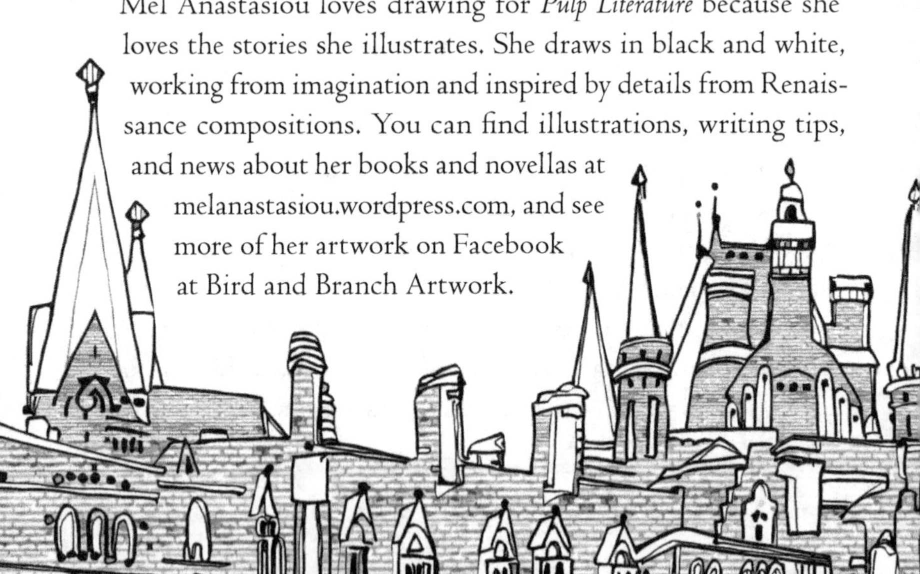

HALL OF FAME

These are the heroes — the Patrons and Pulp Literati whose monthly support helped bring you this issue. Please lift your glasses and give them a rousing cheer!

The Brewers
Robin McGillveray

The Landlords
Dana Tye Rally

The Innkeepers
Ev Bishop
Susan Jackson
Kevin Harris
Gillian Gardiner
Richard Ohnemus
Lorna Ens
Andrea Kepple
Mark Francis
David Jensen
Margot Landels

The Cicerones
Roger & Anne Anastasiou
Jennifer Sommersby

The Bartenders
Alana Krider
Richard Gropp
Ron Graves
Dave Wayne

Scott F Gray
Michelle Balfour
Katriona Greenmoor
KT Wagner
Deepthi Atukorala
Margot Spronk
Margaret Elliott
Peter Halasz
Bjarne Hansen
Leny Wagner
Chris Olee
kc dyer
Brighton Hugg
Bryan Moose
Maureen Cooke
K Anastasiou
Mike Sylvester
Katherine Derbyshire
Rapscallion
Shannon Saunders
Megan Shaw
James Carlino
April DC
Lin & John
   Richardson
Jennifer Getsinger
Finnian Burnett

Anna Belkine
Benjamin Johnson
Suzanne Philip
April DC
Fran Scannell
Jillian Shoichet
Andrea Kirkham
Ernst Pulido
John Olley

The Regulars
Marta Salek
Rina Piccolo
Jenny Blackford
Akemi Art
BC
Meredith Frazier
Catherine Levinson
Vera
Charity Tahmaseb
Marilyn Holt
David Perlmutter
Paul Anguiano
Adam Fout
Rhea Rose
James Gotaas

If you would like to join the ranks of these worthies, you can become a patron on Patreon at patreon.com/pulplit or join the Pulp Literati through our website at pulpliterature.com/join-pulp-literati/.

Out of the fires of a Caribbean slave revolt, shipwrecked on the jungle coast of 16th-century Ecuador, an educated slave, a shaman, and a monk hunted by the Inquisition fight for freedom against the might of Imperial Spain.

Dive into an epic slipstream novel of intrigue and adventure from fantasy author Matthew Hughes, the writer George R.R. Martin calls 'criminally underrated,' and Robert J. Sawyer says is 'a towering talent.'

'A triumph!' - Cecelia Holland
'Sensational' - Candas Jane Dorsey

pulpliterature.com

Fantastic Fresh Fiction!

PULP Literature

Do you have a **story to tell?**
We can help!

Dreamers is dedicated to heartfelt writing. Visit our site for:

- Therapeutic Writing
- Poems & Stories
- Content Marketing
- Creative Nonfiction
- Writing Workshops
- Contests & Anthologies
- Residencies & Retreats
- ...and so much more!

www.DreamersWriting.com

30 yrs of award-winning sci-fi and fantasy

WWW.ONSPEC.CA

In search of a writing community?

Join today!

The Federation of BC Writers is here for you!

- ☑ Workshops/ Webinars
- ☑ Contests
- ☑ Readings
- ☑ Articles

- ☑ Networking
- ☑ Discount Membership for for Students and Seniors

- ☑ Digital Writing Circles
- ☑ Find Inspiration & more!

BRITISH COLUMBIA ARTS COUNCIL | BRITISH COLUMBIA
Supported by the Province of British Columbia

bcwriters.ca/Join

MARKETPLACE

ᴍAGAZINES

Amazing Stories · Back in print! amazingstories.com

The Digest Enthusiast · Digests past & present plus new genre fiction larquepress.com

EVENT Magazine · Poetry & prose eventmagazine.ca

Geist · Ideas + Culture · Made in Canada · geist.com

Mystery Weekly Magazine · The cutting edge of short mystery fiction www.mysteryweekly.com

Neo-opsis · Canadian magazine of science fiction based in Victoria, BC · neo-opsis.ca

OnSpec · The Canadian magazine of the fantastic · onspecmag.wordpress.com

Polar Borealis · Paying market for new Canadian SF&F writers & artists · polarborealis.ca

Room Magazine · Literature, Art & Feminism since 1975 · roommagazine.com

ᴘRINTING & PUBLISHING

First Choice Books/Victoria Bindery Book printing & binding · graphic design · eBooks · marketing materials 1-800-957-0561 · firstchoicebooks.ca

PULP
Literature

The Bumblebee
Flash Fiction Contest
Deadline: 15 February
Prize $300

The Magpie Award for Poetry
Deadline: 15 April
Prize $500

The Hummingbird Flash Fiction Prize
Deadline: 15 June
Prize $300

The Raven Short Story Contest
Deadline: 15 October
Prize $300

The Kingfisher Poetry Prize
Deadline: 15 November
Prize $300

Enter today:
pulpliterature.com/contests

CONTESTS

Pulp Literature runs four annual contests for poetry, flash fiction, and short stories. For contest guidelines, prizes, and entry fees, see pulpliterature.com/contests.

The Bumblebee Flash Fiction Contest
Contest opens: 1 January 2024
Deadline: 15 February 2024
Winner notified: 15 March 2024
Winner published: Issue 43, Summer 2024
Prize: $300

The Magpie Award for Poetry
Contest opens: 1 March 2024
Deadline: 15 April 2024
Winner notified: 15 May 2024
Winner published: Issue 44, Autumn 2024
Prize: $500

The Hummingbird Flash Fiction Prize
Contest opens: 1 May 2024
Deadline: 15 June 2024
Winner notified: 15 July 2024
Winner published: Issue 45, Winter 2025
Prize: $300

The Raven Short Story Contest
Contest opens: 1 September 2024
Deadline: 15 October 2024
Winner notified: 15 November 2024
Winner published: Issue 46, Spring 2025
Prize: $300

EVENT

36th ANNUAL NON-FICTION CONTEST

INCREASED CASH PRIZES
$1,500 • $1,000 • $500

OCTOBER 15

Non-Fiction Contest winners feature in every volume since 1989 and have received recognition from the Canadian Magazine Awards, National Magazine Awards and Best Canadian Essays. All entries considered for publication. Entry fee of $34.95 includes a one-year subscription. We encourage writers from diverse backgrounds and experience levels to submit their work.

eventmagazine.ca

ARC'S POEM OF THE YEAR WINS A GRAND PRIZE OF
$5,000

How to Submit: Enter your poem(s) thru Submittable or via snail mail to PO Box 81060, Ottawa, Ontario, K1P 1B1

Entry Fee: $40 CAD for 1 or 2 poems (or up to 3 poems before the Early Bird deadline), includes a one-year subscription* to *Arc Poetry Magazine*. Additional entries are $5 CAD per poem.

Early Bird Deadline: December 31, 2023
Final Deadline: February 1, 2024

Find more details online at arcpoetry.ca/contests

*one-year subscriptions only available to entrants in Canada. Entrants in the US will receive 2 issues, entrants outside of Canda and the US will receive 1 issue

ARC **POETRY**

$\mathscr{B}$ECOME A PATRON OF PULP LITERATURE

By supporting *Pulp Literature* on Patreon with $2 or more per month, you will be laying the foundation for a secure future for the magazine, as well as ensuring that you never miss an issue! Your subscription includes four big issues of short stories, novellas, poetry, comics, and novel excerpts, delivered to your door or electronic mailbox each year. **Find us at patreon.com/pulplit**

If you prefer to subscribe through our website, go to pulpliterature. com/subscribe.

Or you can send a cheque with the form below to
Subscriptions, Pulp Literature Press, 21955 16 Ave, Langley BC, V2Z 1K5, Canada

Don't miss an issue!

- ❑ **Send me 2 years (8 issues) at the special rate of $110** (save $34)*
- ❑ **Send me 1 year (4 issues) for $60** (save $12)*
- ❑ **Send me 2 years of digital issues for $35** (save $12.92)
- ❑ **Send me 1 year of digital issues for $20** (save $3.96)

Name: ____

Address: ____

City: _________________________________ Prov. / State: _________

Postal code: _______________ Country: ___________________

Email: ____

- ❑ **Payment enclosed**
- ❑ **Bill me**
- ❑ **New**
- ❑ **Renewal**

Make cheques payable in Canadian funds to Pulp Literature Press. Include email address for digital editions and Paypal billing, or subscribe at www.pulpliterature.com/subscribe.

*for postage outside Canada add $20 per year in North America or $32 per year overseas.